MATT'S OATH

A CLASSIC WESTERN

ORRIS SLADE

PROLOGUE

*E*ustace Morley set down the old-fashioned whiskey glass he was polishing and turned toward the sound of the front doors clacking open. The man standing there was tall and broad, and he had the look of a lean hungry wolf. The dust on him from riding fell to the wood floor, and he wasn't someone the restaurant owner recognized.

"Well, howdy, stranger," Eustace called out loud enough for all present in his establishment that afternoon to hear. "You looking for a hot meal? Come on in."

"Much obliged," the newcomer replied, his voice a grating rasp. "Been riding hard and long… A hot meal would be nice, a drink even nicer."

"So where are you from, feller?" Eustace peered at the imposing man as he walked into the restaurant.

"Wyoming," the man replied, keeping the brim of his large black Stetson drawn low over his brow.

"That's quite a while away." Eddie, one of Eustace's able-bodied bouncers, sidled up to the bar counter.

"I reckon it is, friend," the tall stranger said, dusting down his deerskin jacket. "More'n four hunnerd miles. I plumb near rode my horse to death."

"What brings you here to Cripple Creek?" Eustace noted the twin holstered gun belt around the stranger's lean waist as he gestured at a table for the newcomer.

"I hear…" The man took a seat at the table. "There's gold in them thar hills."

"Ain't that the truth?" Eustace nodded. "And work on the upcomin' Florence and Cripple Creek Railroad sure is bringin' a whole lot of new folks into town."

"Good for your viands and vittles business, ain't it?" The Wyoming man grinned. "I'll be having the rump steak, well done. And whiskey by the bottle."

"Business is good for sure." Eustace narrowed his eyes. "And what is your business here in Cripple Creek? You don't look like a miner."

"Why? What does a miner look like?"

"I reckon you look more like a hunter after a bounty…" Eustace shrugged. "I hope you ain't fixin' to rob any of our hard-workin' miners."

"So, you're sayin' I look like a darn outlaw?" The man's grin was wolfish.

"No offense meant, pardner." Eustace smiled defensively. "Just being cautious is all. So, what do they call you back at your homestead?

"No offense taken, friend. Name's Ned." The man leaned back and tapped on the brim of his black Stetson. "So, how's that steak coming along?"

"We serve the best steaks in Cripple Creek." Eustace puffed his chest. "Well done takes its time…"

"Good. Good." Ned took a swig of his whiskey right out of the bottle. "I like my steaks perfect."

"Nothing less." Eustace nodded and stepped back from the

table. "Let me mosey on over to the kitchen and keep an eye on the grillin' myself."

"Yeah. You do that." Ned leaned back on the chair. "Mmm, this is mighty fine whiskey."

The sound of the doors clacking open again drew Eustace's attention once more as he made his way to the kitchen. He grimaced at the sight of the young blond man walking in. Tommy Dawson wasn't the kind of patron Eustace would want in his establishment, but the Dawson ranch had the best steers and thus the best beef his popular restaurant needed.

"Hey, Mister Morley." The Dawson boy, a year short of twenty, was grinning from ear to ear. "Just ran into Big Horace and clipped his darn horns, I did."

"Very nice, Tommy." Eustace sighed. "And what will you be having today… to celebrate?"

"Just a coffee… black, no sugar." Tommy smiled, unholstering and holstering his single-action Smith & Wesson in rapid succession.

"Please quit doing that in here." Eustace leaned over and whispered sharply, "I could do without any goldarn trouble from you for one day."

"Aw, come on, old-timer." Tommy laughed out loud. "There ain't going to be no trouble with me here and my lightning-fast drawing skills."

"Where's Matt?" Eustace asked about the older Dawson boy.

"He's over at the ranch." The younger of the two Dawson boys stifled a yawn. "Pa has him doing some chores around the place… and taking a count of the stock before breeding season."

Eustace sighed in relief. Just the one Dawson boy in today meant just half the usual trouble they made around town. He could live through that.

"Is Becky in today?" Tommy looked eagerly around the dimly lit restaurant for the young waitress. "She makes the best darn coffee…"

"Yup, she's in the kitchen out back…" Eustace replied. "Have a seat, Tommy… I'll go get your coffee. And please don't go troublin' the other customers."

"I never do that, Mister Morley…" Tommy made a face. "I trouble them only when they trouble me first."

If only that were the half of it. Eustace shook his head. The Dawson brothers were two young bucks, naïve and full of piss and vinegar. *They'll learn the hard way that the big bad world doesn't really give two hoots about hotheaded whippersnappers like them. Someday, someone would make them see the error of their ways.* Eustace Morley hoped he wouldn't be anywhere near them when that day ever came.

"Ah, this steak looks mighty fine, darlin'." Eustace heard the newcomer's raspy voice. "Did you cook it all by your purdy lonesome?"

"Er… no," Becky Johnson replied with a quaver in her voice. "I just serve the food… Miss Nellie does the cooking."

"Well, then…" Ned's rasp softened. "I reckon I should be kissing Miss Nellie for this fine meal… but I'd much rather kiss a purdy little thing like you before that."

"Oh, I… I'm flattered for sure, mister." Becky nervously took a step back.

"Hey, where you going, missy?" The newcomer took a grab at her wrist.

"I… I've…" the young woman stammered. "Got other customers to serve."

"Aw, let some other waiter serve 'em," Ned persisted. "You wouldn't let a weary man eat his meal all by his lonesome now, would ya?"

"I'd love to join you, mister." Becky tried to sound indifferent. "But employees can't sit with…"

"Hey, I'm the customer… and I want to share this heavenly steak with you." Ned leaned over his meal. "I'll also leave a nice tip for you…"

"But..." Becky glanced pleadingly over in Eustace's direction. "But mister..."

"Name's Ned, darlin'." Ned laughed gratingly. "What's yours?"

Eustace sighed and shot a quick glance at Tommy. He didn't need this. Not today. Not here and now. Not ever. But it was too darn late. Tommy Dawson was already rising off his chair to dash to Becky's rescue. Eustace jerked his head at his bouncer Eddie and tapped two fingers over his own chest, the signal to go and get the sheriff.

"Well, howdy there, mister?" Tommy's yell was loud enough to make some of the horses tethered outside stamp their hooves. "I don't reckon I've seen you before."

"I don't reckon I've seen you neither," Ned replied with a snarl.

"I see Miss Johnson is taking good care of you this fine afternoon."

"Well, not near good enough..."

"I reckon Becky here has done more than good enough." Tommy fingered the butt of his six-shooter.

"And who might you be, young feller... to be reckonin' that?" Ned's rasp grew colder.

"Aw, pardon my manners, my friend... Tommy Dawson is the name. And I'm the fastest gun in this here town of Cripple Creek."

"Well, that sure is good for you..." Ned tipped the brim of his black hat. "But I ain't got no need for you, boy... so leave a hungry man to his meal and his purdy companion for a while."

"Your purdy companion happens to be my... my friend." Tommy placed his hand on the table, leaning down on it.

"It's all right, Tommy..." Becky all but whispered. "There ain't no need for you..."

"Pshaw, Becky, 'taint no trouble 'tall." Tommy grinned at the pretty young woman.

Eustace gritted his teeth and glanced at the front door. It was always trouble with the Dawson boys. Never a day went without it. And this Ned fellow sure had the look of a mean ornery bastard.

Eddie would need at least five minutes to ride to the sheriff's and another five to get back with the lawman. Anything could happen until then.

"Why don't you get lost, boy." Ned's rasp was a lot harsher. "While you still can…"

"Boy, am I?" Tommy hollered. "You're the stranger in this here town… You don't tell Tommy Dawson what he can do and what he cannot do."

"Tommy, please…" Becky almost wept.

"Get back to the kitchen, Becky." Eustace walked over to the table. "And, Tommy, you'd better leave the man to his meal… before the sheriff gets here."

"You called the sheriff on me, old man…" Tommy glared at Eustace. "On account of this dusty old drifter? Didn't you see him harassing Becky?"

"Ned here wasn't harassing Becky… just asking for her company at his meal."

"And after the meal, what?" Tommy turned toward Ned again. "He was going to give her a big tip… What kind of tip do you reckon that would be?"

Ned's rasping laughter aggravated Eustace, but he didn't want to insult a paying customer. Not just yet. Tommy was right: this stranger was making an obscene pass at Becky. But then almost everyone made a pass at Becky Johnson, one of the prettier young women in Cripple Creek.

"You think that's funny, you old coyote?" Tommy slapped his palm down hard on Ned's table, making the whiskey bottle fall over.

"Careful, boy…" Ned stood up to his full height.

"Or what?" Tommy snarled.

"Or you might regret…"

"I ain't no yellow-belly like old man Morley and his boys here to let a purdy young lady get troubled..." Tommy Dawson growled at the newcomer. "You harassed my Becky... Now you answer to me."

Before Eustace could blink, Tommy upended the table, spilling the contents of Ned's unfinished meal all over the startled man from Wyoming. Tommy's fist followed in next, aimed right at Ned's lean wolfish face.

To the younger man's surprise, he found his clenched fist sailing through empty air. For a tall man, Ned sure was quick on his feet as he ducked and wove away from young Tommy Dawson's wildly flailing fists.

"You stupid crowbait-riding corn cracker." Ned's laughter rang around the eatery as the tall man lashed out with his long leg, catching Tommy at the side of his head.

The dull crack of Ned's booted heel to the young Dawson's temple made Eustace wince as he saw Tommy go down to the ground. But the boy sure had grit and gumption.

He leaped to his feet instantly and dived headfirst into the taller man, making him double up. The two men rolled around on the ground, trading blows and cusswords.

Eustace shook his head ruefully. Those of his customers who hadn't already fled stood at a safe distance, watching the fray. He could see Becky peering out from the half open kitchen door, with Nellie beside her. The sheriff had better get there soon before things got any worse.

"Quick with your fists and feet, are ya?" Tommy frothed at the mouth, a trickle of his blood running down the left side of his head. "How quick are you on the draw?"

The loud discharge of a pistol almost made Eustace's heart leap out of his throat. He expected to see Ned crumpling to the floor. But instead, the tall, lean man was crouched, his pistol aimed at Tommy, still in its holster with the nozzle smoking. He fired without drawing, through the cutaway hole at the bottom of the leather holster. A bold and despicable move.

His mouth hanging open in utter disbelief, Eustace turned to look at Tommy Dawson. The younger of the Dawson boys lay on his back on the wood floor, his hand grasping at the butt of his Smith & Wesson, still in the leather holster.

Tommy's wide eyes, once blue and lively, stared upward in a glassy glaze, even as the dark red spot between them grew bigger.

"He… killed Tommy." Becky's wail broke the deathly silence.

"The sheriff," someone shouted. "Where is the sheriff?"

"You there, Ned… stay where you are." Eustace turned toward the man from Wyoming as he made to leave.

"Are you going to make me… old man?" Ned grinned coldly, and then with leonine grace that defied his size, he dashed out of the eatery.

The sound of a horse neighing outside followed by a rapid clattering of hooves told Eustace the man from Wyoming was on his way out of town.

"Oh no, Tommy." Becky had tears trickling down her flushed cheeks as she knelt beside the fallen man. "Oh, Tommy."

"Garrett Dawson's going to come bearing done here with his posse, soon as he knows," someone said from behind her.

"There'll be hell to pay for this," said another.

"There sure will." Eustace gritted his teeth as Eddie and Sheriff Rawlins, with his deputy Billy, walked into the restaurant.

"What in tarnation…?" The lawman was looking at the lifeless Tommy Dawson.

"Who was that darned scallywag?" Eddie asked no one in particular.

"Did y'all here get a good look at the feller?" the deputy asked.

"Yes, we all did," Eustace replied. "He was tall and lean, really mean lookin'. Said he came riding all the way from Wyoming."

"From Wyoming, eh?" The sheriff rubbed his grizzled chin

and turned to his deputy. "Show these folks the wanted poster, Billy."

"Is this the feller?" Billy unrolled a yellowed paper poster and held it up.

The hand-drawn picture on the wanted poster was almost a close match of the man who was in there enjoying a rump steak not even an hour ago. Though Eustace never got a look at the man's eyes, he was quite certain the picture on the wanted poster was indeed of this Ned.

"Yes, that's him." He nodded at Sheriff Rawlins. "Said his name was Ned."

"That'd be about right." Billy rolled up the poster. "His name is Ned. Ned Shute. And he was on the run from Wyoming... He's wanted there for murder."

"Round up a few men, Billy," Sheriff Rawlins told the deputy, "and ride out after the varmint. I'm going to have to get to the Dawson ranch to give Garrett the news."

"Matt's going to want to go after this Ned Shute himself," Eustace warned the lawman.

"Well, that ain't going to happen." Rawlins lit up a cigarillo. "Not while I am the law in Cripple Creek. Someone get the coroner to take care of Tommy. You, Eustace Morley, you're my prime witness... and you're coming with me to the Dawson ranch."

"But I..." Eustace made to argue but gave in instantly. There was no arguing with Sheriff Jeremiah P. Rawlins. "When are we leaving, Sheriff?"

"Right now."

CHAPTER 1

The sun was on its way down, hovering like a shimmering mirage low on the horizon. The reddish glow of its dying rays cast elongated shadows across the plains.

Matt Dawson dusted down his leather apron and arched his back to ease the stiffness. A hard day's work it sure was. He looked forward to that steak dinner and tequila waiting for him back at the house.

"Looks like someone's riding in hard, Matt." Colby, one of the ranch hands, was peering at the darkening horizon.

"I reckon that looks like more than one." Matt followed Colby's gaze and spat a wad onto the hard-packed ground. "But not enough for an Indian raid."

"There's three of 'em... ridin' as if the devil hisself is on their tail," Eagle-Eye Joe told them, leaping down off the high fence. "And one of 'em's wearin' a golden star."

"The sheriff?" Matt fingered the mahogany handle of his Colt Peacemaker. "What in hell did my idiot brother do now to have the law come tearin' down here?"

He didn't have to wait long to find out, as Sheriff Jeremiah Rawlins and two of his riding companions came into discernable view. He raised his hand, but they had no intention of slowing down.

"Get over to the house, boy," Rawlins called out as the three riders thundered past him. "I got some bad news for your pa."

"What news?" Matt called out as he grabbed the reins of the nearest saddled horse and swung himself up.

The sheriff just gestured at him to follow and kept on riding. Matt kicked his horse into a full gallop and bore down on the three riders. By the time he reached the house, the sheriff and his men were already inside.

"What in tarnation's goin' on?" Matt walked in yelling. "Did Tommy go and kill someone, Sheriff?"

But before the sheriff could reply, Matt felt a chill run down his back. Rawlins and his men had their hats in their hands, and the large frame of Garrett Dawson sat slumped on a chair.

"Pa?" Matt almost tripped on his way to his father. "What in the darndest hell...?"

"It's Tommy, Matt," one of Rawlins's men told him. "He... was shot."

"What?" Matt rounded on the man. "How is... how is he?"

"He didn't make it." Rawlins exhaled deeply. "Tommy's dead. The coroner's on the way here with... his body."

"But... who?" Matt looked at his father and then at the sheriff. "Did you get the bastard who did it? Where is he?"

"No, he got away," Rawlins replied. "Morley here saw the whole thing."

Matt looked at the eldest of the three men for the first time, realizing he was not one of the sheriff's deputies. He remembered him from the restaurant where Becky worked.

"Matt... I..." Eustace Morley began after glancing at Garrett Dawson. "I saw it all..."

"Who was it?" Matt almost demanded.

"A stranger, never saw him before... he... he came in for a meal... and was being fresh with Becky..."

"And Tommy didn't like that," Rawlins cut in.

"Let him tell me." Matt glared at the lawman. "You said he… saw what happened."

"Tommy got into the man's face, and they got into a fist fight," Morley continued. "The guy had Tommy beat, then Tommy made to draw his six-shooter, but Ned… the other guy, shot him first."

"Is that his name? Ned?" Matt looked at the three men standing before him in turns. "Where is he now?"

"He's wanted for murder in Wyoming," the third man spoke up. "Name's Ned Shute. He shot Tommy without drawin' his shootin' iron. Shot him through a cutaway in the holster."

"He… the scoundrel cheated." Matt took in a sharp breath.

"He murdered my son in cold blood." Garrett Dawson stood up to his full towering height and broke his silence. "Which way did he go, Rawlins? Are your men after him?"

"I sent Billy with some good men after the varmint." Rawlins gritted his teeth. "But the feller has a good head start… and its getting dark."

"I'm getting Colby and the boys, Pa." Matt stepped between his father and the sheriff. "We're getting the sonovabi—"

"You'll do no such thing, sonny." Sheriff Rawlins placed his large hand on Matt's sternum and pushed him back. "Not in my jurisdiction. It's my job to bring this murderer to book. Ain't got no time for any wild vendetta. And that goes for you too, Garrett."

"I hear you, Rawlins," Garrett Dawson said coldly. "And I'll let you do your damn job—"

"But Pa…" Matt was aghast at his father's decision. "Tommy… he… but…"

"I know, son…" His father looked at him with fire in his eyes. "But Sheriff Rawlins is right. We must let the law do what they're here for… We have more important things to take care of now."

"Darn right." Sheriff Rawlins nodded. "We do our job better

when regular folks stay out of our way. Tommy… Tommy's body will be here soon. The coroner's carriage is on the way."

"You can mosey on back to town, Rawlins," Dawson, senior, told the lawman. "We can take care of everything from here on. Do your job. Get my son's murderer… none of my boys, and least of all Matt, will bother you."

"Much obliged, Garrett." Rawlins touched the brim of his Stetson. "I will personally let you know as soon as there's more news."

Matt stood seething in silent rage as the lawman and his companions left the house. He walked up to his father as the large man poured himself some bourbon. He was ready for a shouting match with his old man but held himself back as his eyes locked onto his father's. Matt knew what that look meant.

He understood then his father told the sheriff what the sheriff needed to hear. The look in his father's fiery cold eyes told him they would not be waiting around for the law to take care of what was family business.

He took a deep breath and stepped back, feeling a little overwhelmed with everything that was going on.

"The coroner's carriage is here, Mister Dawson," Eagle-Eye Joe announced, peering in through the open front door.

"Help them bring Tommy into the dining hall," Dawson, senior, replied and then turned to Matt. "Get word out to all our kin and neighboring folks, son. And get the preacher here in the morning."

CHAPTER 2

The night was the longest Matt had ever experienced. Sleep was not an option.

The early rays of the new day's sunrise brought little solace for him as he watched members of the family and neighboring folks arrive in somber silence for his brother's last rites.

His jaw clenched, eyes narrowed, and nostrils flaring, Matt stared at his younger brother's body laid under flower wreaths atop the family dining table.

The lump he felt in his throat ever since he saw them bring Tommy's body off the carriage never seemed to go down, and neither did the knot in his belly abate. He closed his eyes and exhaled heavily as a family member sobbed next to him.

Matt would never hear Tommy's laugh again. Nor the naïve and stupid things the fool boy would often say. He would never wrestle with his kid brother again, and never have the shooting matches they had, making empty cans of beans and bone-dry whiskey bottles fly off the fence.

His knees trembled, yet he held on to his resolve. Matt was hurting inside, but he would never show that on the outside.

"Tommy," he thought somberly, "I'll get the bastard for you, little brother. I'll send him to hell with six blue whistlers in his head."

He glanced at his father as family and friends milled around the large man, offering their condolences. The old preacher cleared his throat and gestured for silence as he held the Bible in his bony hands. The men stood upright and kept their heads low, their hats in their hands, and the ladyfolk drew their veils low over their bowed heads.

"No one lives for oneself, and no one dies for oneself." The preacher's melodious voice resonated across the crowded room. "For if we live, we live for the Lord, and if we die, we die for the Lord; so then, whether we live or die, we are the Lord's."

"Amen!" voices chorused solemnly all around.

"The Lord is my shepherd; I shall not want," Preacher Watkins continued. "He maketh me to lie down in green pastures: he leadeth me beside the still waters…"

Matt found his mind wandering. He pictured himself tracking down and cornering his brother's killer. He imagined himself shooting the gun that killed Tommy clean out of the man's hand and then firing the rest of his bullets into the killer's pleading face.

No mercy. No mercy at all.

"Surely goodness and mercy shall follow me all the days of my life." The preacher's powerful voice soared, piercing into Matt's thoughts. "And I will dwell in the house of the Lord forever."

"Amen!" the chorus echoed again.

The ranch hands carried the coffin outside, behind the barn, by the old oak where all the deceased of the Dawson family of Cripple Creek were buried. Matt helped them in the heart-breaking task, all the while thinking of how he would avenge Tommy.

The preacher said another prayer as they filled in the earth and planted a small cross at the head of the grave.

"I'll get him for you, Tommy," Matt whispered under his

breath amid the prayer. "Even if I have to ride to the darn ends of this Earth, I'll get the sonovabitch and make him pay."

* * *

"I know Rawlins, Matt," his father told him. "He ain't goin' to let up on his promise... to keep us from getting our own justice."

"It ain't right, Pa." Matt gritted his teeth as he listlessly prodded at the ground beef patty on his place, his appetite never there. "A man's in his right to seek vengeance on the ones who wronged him."

"That sure is the truth, son..." Garrett Dawson pushed away his own half-eaten plate of food. "And we Dawsons take care of our own... but we have to be extra careful with Rawlins's eagle eye on us... We've got to be real discreet about this."

"You leave this to me, Pa." Matt exhaled deeply. "I'll track this maggot down myself... I'll do it alone, no need to trouble any of our boys... and on my own, I'll attract less attention."

"You have to be careful, boy... real careful." Dawson, senior, held his bourbon glass to his lips. "I ain't keen on losing another son anytime too soon."

"Rest easy on that, Pa." Matt gave his father a look of determination. "I ain't no kid like Tommy... I'm not going to..."

"You boys were too cocky for your own good. Going around town, swaggering and drawing your guns, willy-nilly..."

"Best you don't go there, Pa..." Matt shook his head, his ears burning. "It's different now. Tommy's dead. I aim to get that bastard... I'm going to track him down and kill him in cold blood, like he did Tommy."

"It's going to be tough, son." Garrett gave him a look of concern. "I reckon you could use Colby and Eagle-Eye's experience and help."

"That'd be real good, Pa. But I'll have to do this alone, and you need to keep that darned Rawlins distracted."

"Yep, I can keep that old lawman off your back." Dawson, senior, nodded slowly. "And you'd better outfit yourself with the best guns and carry more than enough bullets, ya hear?

"Don't worry on that count, Pa." Matt stood up and patted his heavy gun belt. "My pair o' Colts here and Grandpa's old shotgun is more than enough lead for me to send that varmint to hell a few times over."

"Confidence is good, son." Garrett Dawson stood up and patted him on his shoulders. "But too much of it ain't goin' to work for you. It didn't do Tommy no good."

"I'll keep that in mind, Pa."

"Where you goin' to start lookin', son?"

"The place where it happened," Matt said as he turned to leave. "Eustace Morley's eatin' house."

"I better get the boys do something to get Rawlins out of town for a while."

"I reckon that would be just fine," Matt called out as he walked out of the house. "See you soon, Pa."

CHAPTER 3

"Oh, Matt!" Becky's wide eyes were red rimmed from crying. "I told him... I told Tommy to let it go, but he..."

"It's ain't your fault, Becky." Matt stared into her blue eyes but more with concern than the usual look of desire he had for her. "That man's a wanted killer... if not Tommy, he'd have killed someone else... it's in their darned nature..."

"What're you goin' to do, Matt?" she whispered, the fear evident in her trembling voice.

"I'm fixin' to find the sonovabitch..." Matt replied coldly. "And avenge Tommy."

"But that man..." Becky touched his forearm. "He shot his gun so quick... Tommy didn't even draw..."

"That bastard cheated." Matt took a sip of his whiskey. "He shot his gun through a hole cut in the holster. That's a coward's act... a low, despicable act."

"I'm so scared, Matt," Becky whimpered. "I never felt so horrified before... seeing Tommy fall..."

"Been hard on all of us, Becky..." Matt gave her a little smile. "It's all right to feel scared."

"Matt Dawson?" he heard someone softly call out his name.

Turning his head slowly, he looked at the tall, slender man standing behind his chair. "Howdy, Deputy Grant?" Matt smiled slightly.

"The sheriff told me to keep an eye out for you," Billy Grant said haltingly.

"And why in thunderation did he tell you to do that, Deputy?" Matt took a slow sip of his drink. "Am I an ornery outlaw now?"

"Um… er… no, but…" The deputy, almost as young as Matt himself, seemed to redden. "Just that the sheriff…"

"Where'n the sam hill is Sheriff Rawlins?" Matt pushed, sensing the young man's discomfort at being contested. Deputy Billy Grant would have a lot to learn if he ever wanted to become sheriff someday.

"He's… out of town," Billy replied cautiously. "Some trouble near the Hogan ranch."

"That's way over the eastern ridge, a few hours hard riding, I'd reckon." Matt nodded with a smirk. "So why does Sheriff Rawlins want you to keep your eye on me?"

"He said… you might make trouble… here in town."

"Matt's here to see me, Deputy." Becky reached out to touch the junior lawman's arm. "We all miss Tommy."

"I… I…" Billy Grant took a step back. "Sure thing, Miss Johnson. Sorry to bother you, Mr. Dawson. I'll leave you two now. Carry on."

Matt touched the brim of his hat in acknowledgement as the young deputy turned on his heel and walked away. It would have served him better had he stuck to silently watching Matt instead of walking over to tell him about it. A greenhorn mistake and Billy Grant would surely learn from it.

"So, we know the sheriff and his boys are really sticking to their promise to make it hard for me go after my brother's killer." Matt didn't hide the disdainful snicker. "All the more reason that I have to do this then."

"But how're you goin' to find that gosh-awful man?"

"I'll find him, Becky." Matt took her small soft hands in his large rough ones. "I'll ride the length and breadth of this country, even if it takes a coon's age… I'll find that mangy polecat and fill him full of lead plumbs."

"Oooh! You're goin' to… kill him?" Her eyes were as wide as a little girl seeing her first rainbow.

"I reckon that'll be sweet justice for my little brother."

"But Sheriff Rawlins said…"

"Doesn't matter what that ornery ol' leather face said, Becky…" Matt took a deep breath. "A man's gotta do what a man's gotta do, and this… I've got to do."

"But what if… this outlaw is too much for you?" Becky held on to his hands tightly. "I'm so scared somethin' bad will happen to you…"

"I'm not Tommy, Becky," Matt told her softly. "Tommy was still too young. I'm a man full grown… I know my responsibility."

"I pray to God you know what you're doing, Matt." Becky had a tear in her eye. "I'm so heartbroken over Tommy… I don't think I can live if anything bad happens to you."

"Ain't nothin' bad goin' to happen to me, Becky…" Matt stood up. "All the bad's goin' to this feller Ned Shute. I gotta go now, Becky. I'll see you when I get back."

"Oh, Matt." Becky leaned in close. "Promise me you'll come back quick."

"I promise you, Becky…" Matt's lips almost brushed hers. "I'll come back quick for you…"

The scent of her golden hair made him feel a little light-headed. The warmth of her breath on his lips almost made him want to not do this. She leaned in and kissed him on the lips.

Matt felt a jolt go through him. He wanted the kiss to go on forever, but his head overruled his heart.

He held Becky by her slender shoulders and pulled away. Her

blue eyes were glimmering with fresh tears. He tore his gaze away and pulled his Stetson lower on his brow.

"I gotta go," he mumbled and turned around on his heel. Matt walked out quickly, not looking back at her. On his way out of the restaurant, he passed a very bewildered-looking Eustace Morley as the owner came in with the day's groceries.

CHAPTER 4

The sun was high in the sky, but the wind that whipped across his face was cool. Matt shot a glance back at the way he had come. He was no expert at tracking, but he understood trails well enough to know which ones were best used for quickly moving through an area.

If he were a man trying to get away from a populated place, he would surely take the road that would get him out of town the quickest.

It had been almost forty-eight hours now since Ned Shute had run out of Cripple Creek. The sheriff's men who had chased after him returned empty handed the night before. He didn't want to let another search party going after Shute before he did.

The rundown little tavern he had been staring at for a while now could be a good place to get some information, he reckoned.

Matt eased his young gelding down the cutaway slope toward the ramshackle little saloon on the edge of the creek. There'd be just a few people there at this time of day. Most of them would be all over the hills, scouring for gold.

A heavyset bald-headed man stepped out of the saloon to spit a wad of tobacco into the horse trough outside. Matt had a good mind to charge his horse over and run the scalawag down. But the trough was dry and matched the sorry state of the saloon it was a part of.

He dismounted and tethered his horse, even as the tobacco spitter ignored him, belched and walked back inside through the rickety little doors.

Matt followed the man in. The place was worse inside than it was outside. The tables barely had enough legs to keep standing. And the chairs were the same, with most of them lacking backrests.

He could tell this place has seen a fair amount of violence by all the bullet holes in the walls and furniture. It didn't matter to him if it served his purpose.

"Howdy!" Matt called out to the bored-looking bartender. "The name's Dawson… I need some information."

"Where you from, mister?" The lanky bartender looked at him with glassy, disinterested eyes.

"The Dawson ranch up north," he said, pulling up a creaking stool to the bar counter. "And what do I call you, pardner?"

"Name's Poe." The man yawned. "You want a drink? All we got is rotgut."

"It's information I want, Poe." Matt fished out the wanted poster of Ned Shute that Becky had spirited away from the deputy for him. "Have you seen this feller?"

Poe narrowed his baggy eyes and scratched his large nose. "Maybe. Are you one of the sheriff's deputies?"

"No."

"Well, if you don't have a shiny star on, I don't have to tell you nothing." Poe grinned through blackened teeth. "And you can slide, mister."

"I have other shiny things…" Matt glanced back over his shoulder at the heavyset tobacco spitter seated at the far corner of the saloon. "I can give you, Poe."

"What kind of shiny things?" A hint of greed glazed over Poe's dullish eyes.

"Gold, if you tell me what I want to know." Matt fingered the dark mahogany handle of his Colt Peacemaker. "Or a shiny blue whistler between the eyes if you try to sour my milk."

"I know him," Poe said. "He's a wanted man."

"Is that right?" Matt leaned in closer. "Is that why they put his purty face on the wanted poster? Tell me more, consarn it."

"Ay, I'm an honest businessman, you can't…"

In a blur of movement, Matt had his pistol pointed at the flustered man's large nose. "I ain't got time for jawin', pardner. Either you tell me what I need to know, and I toss you a piece of gold, or I leave you with a third nostril."

"Honest to God, man." Poe raised his bony hands over his face. "Is all I know. He's an outlaw… a horse thief… and… and a… a murderer."

"Was he here?"

"I… yes, yes… he was."

"When was it?" Matt pressed the cold steel of his Colt barrel on the barman's nose.

"Two days ago." Poe swallowed hard. "He was in a hurry… grabbed a few flasks of rotgut… and left."

"Did he say where he was headin'?"

"He said nothing… he nary even paid for the hooch."

"You're lyin' again, Poe." Matt cocked back the hammer.

"No… no…" The man shivered visibly. "Don't shoot… I… yeah… he said something about riding south…"

"Where south?"

"The border… New Mexico border."

"If you're lying, Poe…" Matt lowered his pistol. "You better not be here when I come back."

"I ain't lying…" Poe took a quick gulp of his own wares. "Shute's headed for New Mexico."

"The border of New Mexico is more than two hundred miles

from here…" Matt rubbed his two-day stubble. "That's almost a ten-day ride, five if he wants to kill his horse."

"You can beat him, if you want to kill yours," Poe offered with a nervous grin.

"Did you see the horse he was riding?"

"No. But I reckon he can change horses on the way…" the lanky barman replied. "One dies on him; he can steal another… The man's a dam horse thief."

"I won't outrun him, but I'm sure to rights he'll be holin' up there for a while." Matt walked slowly back toward the clacking saloon doors. "I'll find that polecat when I'm there…"

"What're you after him for if you ain't a lawman?" Poe called after him. "Did he kill anyone you know?"

"Something like that," Matt said and walked out of the decrepit place.

CHAPTER 5

Three days since he had set off for the southern border, and he wasn't pleased with the slow progress. In three days, he'd covered just a quarter of the way, but he didn't want to kill his horse by running it into the ground. Half his supplies of jerky and cornbread remained, and he had seven more days of riding to do.

"I reckon there'll be a farmstead up the road," he told himself. "Might get some food and drink."

He rode on slowly, his horse cantering at a steady pace, preserving his strength to cover more ground. He patted the laboring animal's neck every now and then, whispering soothing words of encouragement to keep him going.

Matt loved this horse and all the horses at the Dawson ranch. He could never ever imagine running down one of these magnificent beasts to their death.

He looked up at the sky. The sun had already begun its westward dip down. Day six since Tommy's unfortunate demise. He cursed under his breath, quelling the sudden urge to kick the horse into a full gallop. No, never.

He chided himself just as he heard the familiar whinny of

another horse up ahead. The gelding was just as excited as he was and broke into a trot toward the source of the other animal.

"Easy there, boy." Matt patted the horse's neck gently. "Easy… we'll get there soon enough."

The farmland before him was sparse and dust ridden as the horse trotted along the beaten path. Then he saw it: the other horse that had made that frantic cry. It seemed to be distraught. Its rider was having a hard time staying on the saddle as the horse stomped and kicked around.

Gently, Matt kicked his gelding into a light gallop, closing in on the hapless rider. He realized the rider was too small to be a man. A boy? No, a girl.

A dark-haired young girl, and frightened as she was, she still had the gumption to hold on to the reins and saddle, even as her horse bucked and kicked, stirring up a dust cloud all around it.

"Hey there, missy?" he called out to get her attention. "What's spooked your horse?"

The young girl looked in his direction in surprise. She hadn't noticed him riding up. Releasing the reins from her right hand, she pointed to the ground and said, "Rattlers."

Sure enough, the horse was trampling down on three of the deadly reptiles even as they writhed and coiled under its hooves, tails rattling and fangs dripping with venom.

Calm as the summer breeze, Matt drew the mahogany-handled Colt Peacemaker from his left holster and fired three shots in succession. The rattling sound stuttered and then completely died down. "Them devils are dead, miss." He holstered his gun.

"Oh, thank you, sir," the girl replied with a gasp as she finally managed to calm her horse. "You saved my life."

"Any decent feller would have done the same, miss." He tipped his hat to her. "Are you… from this here farm?"

"Oh…" She looked at him with wary eyes. "I am… yes. This is our farm."

"I need some supplies. Bread, beans… some beef jerky. I'll pay well for it," he told the girl. "My name's Dawson. I'm from Cripple Creek."

"Oh, um… you'll need to talk to my pa about the supplies," she said as her horse finally calmed down and began grazing. "The house is a mile that way."

"What were you doing out here by yourself?" Matt asked her. She looked about sixteen. A pretty lass with dark hair and large green eyes.

"Most of our farmhands ran off north, to the hills…" the girl said she as eased her horse to a canter beside him.

"For the gold rush…" He nodded knowingly. A few of the Dawson ranch men had run off to try their luck at the mines.

"Yep. I reckon everyone wants to get rich quick…"

"And what about your pa?" he asked her. "And your brothers?"

"Pa's all I got. Never had any brother." She sighed deeply. "So, Pa needs me to ride around the farm now every afternoon…"

"And your ma?"

"God took her when I was little," she said with a shrug. "My pa's new wife don't like me much."

"She's still new?"

"This one is," the girl replied. "Pa married three more times after my ma went."

Matt shuddered a bit at the thought of marrying four times. "You didn't tell me your name."

"Oh, I plumb forgot, being so scared and all," she said, almost blushing. She looked very pretty then. "Pa calls me Katie."

"That's a pretty name."

"And what's your name?"

"I'm Dawson."

"Yep, you said you're Dawson from Cripple Creek." Katie nodded. "But what's *your* name?"

"You're a clever girl." He smiled at her. "My pa named me Matt."

"You're very handsome, Matt." She blushed again. "Thank you again for saving Gully and me."

"Gully?" Matt mused. "Oh, the horse."

"Yep." She nodded. "And what's your horse's name? He's handsome too."

"My horse… doesn't have a name."

"For shame." She shook her head. "He's very beautiful. Such a purty color too. You should give him a name."

"I'm plumb stupid at coming up with names, Katie." Matt rubbed his palm over his face, feeling quite good after a long while, having this idle chatter with a docile stranger. "Can you think of a name for him?"

"Dark Lightning is what I think you should call him." Katie shrugged. "He looks very strong and fast, and his coat is so dark and shiny."

"Done." He laughed softly. "I name him Dark Lightning from this day forth."

"We're almost at the house," Katie told him. "My pa can tell you about the supplies you'd be wanting."

Before Matt could reply, the loud report of a shotgun being fired into the air made both horses rear up and whinny.

"Katie!" A deep voice followed the sound of the buckshot. "Katie! Get away from that man."

"Pa!" The girl turned around, visibly surprised.

Matt followed her gaze, years of practice making him instantly reach for his guns.

Walking very slowly up to them was a large bear of a man, his face red and eyes white with rage. The bearskin coat he wore gave him more the appearance of the animal he resembled. He ejected the spent shell of his shot gun and pumped it again before aiming it right at Matt.

"You!" the man yelled at Matt. "Get back. Stay away. Turn your horse around and get the sam hill away from here."

"Pa!" Katie yelled back at the man.

"Hush!" he shouted over her. "Get back to the house, girl…"

"No, Pa!" The slender girl outyelled the huge man. "You listen to me, Pa. He saved my life."

"What?" The bearskin coat-wearing giant was taken aback.

"He saved my life, Pa." Katie said with a deep breath, "He shot three rattlers, faster'n I could see."

CHAPTER 6

The farmhouse was a large log structure, built well enough to keep the heat out in the summer and the cold from blowing in the winter. Matt was impressed by the handiwork that went into building this decades-old homestead.

"You're from the Dawson ranch?" Katie's father asked him.

"Yup." Matt nodded as they entered the house. "You know the place?"

"Hear of it often when I go up the creek to deliver my produce," the large man replied as he grabbed a half-filled flask of rotgut from the kitchen shelf. "Good beef is what I hear they sell."

"We take pride in our beef." Matt smiled. "I'm Matt Dawson."

"Name's Coolidge." The other man poured two tin cups and pushed one across the wood table at him. "What brings you here, Matt Dawson?"

"Lookin' for someone," he said with a sip.

"A wife?" Coolidge eyed him suspiciously. "My Katie's not yet of age."

"No, not lookin' for a wife." Matt almost laughed. "Not yet."

"Good call. You're young yet." The larger man nodded. "Who're you lookin' for?"

"This feller." Matt unfolded the wanted poster of Ned Shute. "Seen the scalawag?"

Coolidge narrowed his eyes at the poster and then looked up at Matt. His dark eyes held recognition, but he tried to hide it, Matt could tell. "Are you a marshal?"

"No." Matt shook his head slowly.

"What do you want with this feller?" The farmer leaned back on his creaking chair.

"He a friend of yours?"

"Never seen him before." Coolidge looked away.

"Your eyes tell me otherwise, mister." Matt calmly took another sip of his drink.

"All right, yes, I saw him." Coolidge sighed deeply and drained his cup. "He was here a couple days ago, wantin' supplies, same as you… only he didn't offer to pay."

"And what did you do?"

"I reckoned he was an outlaw, and I wanted no trouble… no trouble for my Katie." The large man slumped his broad shoulders. "So, I gave him what he wanted and let him be on his way."

"Did he say where he was headed?"

"No. But he rode south." Coolidge smoothed down his graying beard. "Reckon he's headin' for New Mexico."

"You might be right." Matt nodded as he stared at the golden liquid in the tin cup he held.

"What are you after him for?"

"The same." Matt sipped his rotgut. "He took something from me."

"You're a young feller." Coolidge looked at him hard. "You sure you have the grit to take a man like that down?"

"I reckon I do."

"I reckon a posse would give you better odds."

"I work best alone." Matt put the empty cup down on the wood table.

"That's what all the young ones say, until they're six feet

under." Coolidge shook his head. "You need more experience, boy... You need learnin' from men who have been doin' what you're settin' out to do."

"I'm much obliged for your advice, mister, and the whiskey." Matt stood up, memories of Tommy rushing into his mind. "Now about the supplies?"

"I got some in the back." The large farmer rose to his feet. "Cornbread, hard cheese, jerky, beans and a couple flasks of rotgut."

"Sounds good." Matt reached into his broad belt, fished out a leather pouch, and tossed it at Coolidge. "That should cover it."

Coolidge hefted the pouch in his large hand and nodded with satisfaction at the familiar sound of coins jingling before gesturing at Matt to follow him into the back room. There were plenty of supplies there for an entire army to last a month.

The Coolidge farm must be doing well, Matt figured. But they'd need the farmhands back from the gold rush to keep the good harvest going.

Matt collected what he paid for. "Much obliged," he told the farmer as he carried the supplies out of the room. "Your quantities are mighty generous."

"You earned that, for saving my Katie's life." The large man nodded somberly.

"I would reckon you don't send her out doin' that kind of work again," Matt replied. "Or at least ride together with her."

"I reckon I'll be doin' just that," Coolidge said as he stepped back into the supply room. "God speed, young feller."

The fresh supplies would last him through the week's ride down south, Matt reckoned as he loaded his saddlebags. The wind was picking up, making tiny dust devils swirl around in the distance.

He mounted his horse and turned to face the sound of running footsteps behind him, his hand instinctively lowering to his holster.

"You're leaving, Matt Dawson of Cripple Creek?" Katie Coolidge panted as she caressed the gelding's shiny coat.

"Got what I needed," he told her, patting his loaded saddlebag. "Reckon I'd best be on my way before dark."

"I want to thank you again for saving me and Gully from them rattlers," the girl said.

"Just did what's right, miss." He smiled at her.

"I'll miss Dark Lightning." She leaned in and kissed the gelding's cheek. "And I'll miss you, Matt Dawson."

"You be careful now, you hear," Matt told her as he gently kicked his horse into a trot. "Stay away from the dry fields."

"Goodbye, Matt Dawson." The girl almost had a sob in her voice.

Matt tipped his hat to her and urged Dark Lightning into a full gallop down the trail heading south.

CHAPTER 7

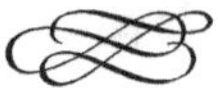

$\mathcal{I}$t had been six days now since Matt had crossed into the mostly arid northern countryside of New Mexico on the trail of his brother's murderer. Almost half a month since Tommy was shot dead in cold blood.

The town of Willow Springs loomed up before him just before noon as Dark Lightning kept a steady canter going. Matt was certain Shute would be holed up in Willow Springs.

The town was growing quickly and was known for its excesses when it came to gambling and other sinful pleasures. Willow Springs seemed like the perfect setting for someone like Ned Shute to make a killing or two.

Another hour of riding had him well within the town. Not all that much different from Cripple Creek, the town of Willow Springs had a certain feel of lawlessness about it. Matt was even more assured he would find Shute here and send him to his maker.

The first of the town's saloons, Fat Farley's, came into view, and Matt eased the tan gelding up to the tethering post and horse trough.

"Stay here, boy," he whispered to the lathered beast as he slung the reins over the post. "I'll be right out."

Piano music greeted him as he stepped inside Fat Farley's Saloon through the swinging butterfly doors. The place was alive, even at this early time of the day.

Matt walked up to the bar counter and pulled up a three-legged stool. He tipped his hat at each of the pretty young ladies sitting at the counter to his left and his right. Their painted smiles grew even wider as their dark eyes remained on him.

Matt was accustomed to the inviting looks he got from the fairer sex. He was young yet and rather good looking. But now, he had more important things on his mind.

He turned to the skinny bartender as the hatchet-faced man approached him.

"Whiskey?" the man asked insipidly.

"Yup." Matt gave the man a grin. "And some information."

"Whiskey's three cents a glass." The bartender leaned in closer. "And ten times that for whatever it is you'll be askin' about."

"Fine by me, pardner. Now pour me some bourbon."

"Best bourbon in the territory for wetting your whistle." The man poured him the drink. "And what else?"

"I'm lookin' for a man." Matt kept his tone low and flat. "A wanted man… wanted for murder in two states, could be more."

"We get all types in here, pardner." The bartender matched his emotionless tone. "You got a name…"

"I got a name and a picture," Matt replied as he sipped the whiskey. "Name's Shute, Ned Shute."

"Not heard of no Ned Shoot. Show me the picture."

Matt slipped out the wanted poster and unfolded it. He watched for the man's reaction. Sure enough, the barman's eyes gave away the truth. Shute was known here. Maybe he was still in Willow Springs.

"I know him." The barman nodded, much to Matt's surprise. He'd expected the man to deny the fact.

"Where is he?" Matt eyed the man keenly.

"Don't know that, but I seen him around town."

"Did he come in here?"

"Sure, he does almost every evenin' when the big boys begin their poker game."

"So, he'll be in here today?"

"Can't tell." The barman snorted. "If he's on a wanted poster, the man's an outlaw… He can be here today and gone tomorrow.'

"There a sheriff in this town?" Matt shot a quick glance over either shoulder.

"Sure is."

"Why ain't he apprehendin' a wanted man?" Matt drained his drink and set the empty glass on the counter,

"You could ask that to the sheriff y'self." The barman poured him another glass of bourbon. "Or maybe this Shute feller isn't a wanted man here in Willow Springs."

"Makes it easier for me then, I reckon."

"Whatever it is you're lookin' for with this feller for is none of my business." The barman leaned in even closer. "But I seen the feller shoot, he's quicker'n most eyes can see… You'd best be warned."

"Much obliged, pardner." Matt tipped his hat.

"Better when you pay up." The barman held out his hand. "Six cents for the bourbon, and sixty for all the jawin' you made me do."

"You earned it, pardner." Matt slapped the money onto the man's open palm. "And there's more if you're in the mood to jaw again."

"Come back here, later in the evenin'," the barman said and moved on toward another customer at the far end of the bar. "I just might have more jawin' to do."

"Well, well… who's this tall, dark handsome stranger we have here, Lilly?" A sweet lilting voice from his left made Matt slowly turn on the barstool.

"Can't tell, Molly," a voice to his right replied. "Never seen him before… I would have remembered if I had, judgin' by the dashin' looks on him."

"Ladies." Matt tipped his hat to the two young women seated on either side of him. "What can I do for you?"

"Well, seein' you're here all by your lonesome, we reckon a big young lad like you could use some of what Lilly and I have to offer." The blue-eyed blond called Molly bit her rose-red lips.

"Yep, you just hit the jackpot, cowboy…" Lilly, the redhead, purred as seductively as her companion. "The two of us together… for the price of one."

"I'm real flattered by this generous offer, ladies…" Matt leaned back onto the bar counter. "But I'm here in town on a different kind of business… Just ain't got the time for nothin' else."

"Ah, that's such a pity," Lilly went on, making big doe eyes at him. "We'd reckon you could afford the full service… seeing how much you paid for your drinks."

"I'm afraid, ladies… I just don't have the time to spare."

"Maybe you could buy a girl one drink." Molly got close enough for him to catch a whiff of the heady scent in her hair.

"Sure, I reckon I can do that." Matt nodded and turned toward the bartender. "Two glasses of bourbon for the two ladies, pardner."

"That'll be six cents." The man placed the drinks before the smiling women.

"I'll settle that later in the evenin'… when I'll be back for some more of your jawin'." Matt got up to leave. "Tell me, where I can find a good barber here?"

"Two blocks down, by the undertaker's," the bartender said as Matt walked out the swinging doors.

CHAPTER 8

The evening breeze was much cooler, and the shave and wash he got at the barber's had Matt feeling clean and refreshed. Thirteen days in the saddle through dust-ridden trails was no better than the cattle drives Matt had been on for the ranch.

He headed back for Fat Farley's Saloon. He was certain the bartender would have a lot more to tell him, for the right price.

He tethered his gelding to the post and walked in through the swinging doors. The place was even livelier than earlier, and the piano music had a beat you could dance to. On the raised platform beside the piano player, several young women were dancing an Irish jig, long shapely legs kicking upward and billowy skirts flying high.

The tables were all full, and men and women milled around. On almost every table, men were holding their cards in grubby hands close to their chests, placing bets and drinking whiskey.

Matt scanned the packed room slowly. Ned Shute could be here. He wondered how he would do it once he spotted the man. Should he just walk up and shoot him, or should he call him outside and challenge him to a fair duel?

Either way, Matt knew he had to bolt like a bat out of hell after the act. He wasn't keen on getting hanged in Willow Springs accused of murder.

"Is he here?" he asked softly, walking up to the hatchet-faced bartender.

"Who?" The man eyed him furtively.

"Shute."

"Shute?" The skinny man feigned ignorance.

"The man we were talkin' about earlier today," Matt said through gritted teeth.

"What in tarnation are you jawin' about, pardner?"

"Cut the bull crap." Matt slapped down a few coins on the wood counter. "Here's the six cents I owe you for the whiskey. Now pour me another."

"Ah, yup." The man almost grinned. "It's all a-comin' back to me now… Memory ain't as good as it used to be, y'know."

"I reckon it ain't when it suits you." Matt took a sip. "Now, tell me what else you know. If it's useful, it'll be worth a whole dollar to you."

"Oh, yep, yep." The man leaned closer and nodded. "Sure is goin' to be useful, goldarn it, it sure is."

"Keep talkin'."

"This Shute feller, he's goin' to be down at the town blacksmith, over by the southern gate of town."

"When?"

"Around nine," the bartender replied after glancing to the left and then the right.

"What about?"

"I hear he's fixin' to rob the bank," the man whispered sharply.

"Is he meetin' someone at the blacksmith?"

"Word is he's lookin' for men to join him for the heist."

"And the sheriff has no inklin' of this?" Matt gave the man a doubtful look.

"Sheriff's out of town, trouble down by the Santa Fe Trail…
stagecoach bein' robbed and all."

"So, Shute's been waitin' for this… to rob the bank when the
sheriff's away."

"Bingo, pardner." The grin on the man's hatchet face was as
bland as a dead fish. "You catch on quick. Darn clever of you."

"Pour me another and spare me the brownnosin'."

"Sure thing." The bartender refilled Matt's glass. "All that's
worth the dollar, I reckon."

"After you give me directions to the blacksmith."

"Got any paper and pencil?"

"Here." Matt fished out the wanted poster and a piece of
charcoal.

"There you go, pardner." The barman drew a few rough boxes
and lines on the back of the poster and handed it back. "Best get
there before nine."

"Much obliged." Matt drained the glass of bourbon and
slapped a dollar and twenty cents on the counter. "I'll be back if
you aren't being on the level."

"Oh, I am on the level." The other man quickly palmed the
coins. "Swear on the almighty."

CHAPTER 9

Matt stood beside the tall clock tower by the town hall. The clock's hour hand was almost on the nine, and the longer minute hand moved with a dull click closer to the ten.

He had ten minutes to make it back to the blacksmith's by the southern gate. Having already ridden by the place an hour earlier, Matt knew the way and was in no hurry. He let his horse slowly trot on.

He dismounted a few yards away from the blacksmith and caressed Dark Lighting's brow.

"Stay here, boy… stay very, very quiet," Matt whispered softly at the gently nuzzling horse. "I'm goin' to need you to run like the devil himself was on our tail once I get the deed done."

This part of Willow Springs was less populated. Just the town blacksmith and horseshoe maker's buildings stood before the south gate. Further up to the center of town were the town hall and the church.

Matt had toured the entire town earlier in the evening, noting the layout and mapping a way to leave town in a hurry, which he was certain he would have to do once he got Shute.

The blacksmith's was closed. No lights lit and no sound. Just as it was an hour ago when he rode by. This looked a perfect place for outlaws to hunker down and plan a robbery.

Matt walked cautiously up to the gloomy-looking building, his fingers idly caressing the mahogany handles of his twin Colt Peacemakers.

The clock at the town center struck nine. Matt stood before the locked door of the blacksmith, his eyes keenly scanning the area for the man he'd been hunting for more than two weeks.

A soft crunch of boots on gravel behind him made Matt draw his left pistol. He turned slowly, Colt Peacemaker at his hip aimed high.

"Easy, feller." A low but gruff voice greeted him.

The tall form of a man wearing all black was silhouetted by the dim light from the southern gate watchtower. The man reached into his breast pocket, drew a cigarillo to his lips, and lit it.

Matt caught a glimpse of the man's face in the brief flash of light. He wasn't the one on the wanted poster Matt had.

"You here for the job, pardner?" the man asked him as he blew a smoke circle.

"Depends on what the job is?" Matt kept his gun trained on the man.

"I reckon you've been told," the other replied. "Reason why you're here?"

"I'm here for Ned Shute."

"Never heard the name."

"I was told… he needs men… for the job," Mat said slowly, forcing himself to be patient.

"You mean the boss." The man titled his head.

"Yep. I mean him."

"Yeah, he's at the back."

"Back? Where?" Matt glanced at the dark silhouette of the blacksmith's building.

"Back there." The man pointed behind the blacksmith's with his lit cigarillo.

"Anyone else coming?"

"Maybe." The other nodded and blew out another puff of smoke. "You go on back there, meet the boss. I'll be waiting here for anyone else comin' for the job."

"Okay. I'm headin' on back." Matt nodded, his gun still in his hand. If Ned Shute was there, behind the blacksmith's building, it would be easier for him to do what he came for and bolt out of town through the south gate.

Rounding the dark corner, Matt stepped over several discarded pieces of ore and melted iron and tin scraps. He stepped on some hardened lumps, his boot twisting at the ankle, making him grunt in pain.

"Watch your step, pardner," someone standing right before him growled.

He looked up, his feet unsteady, his instinct making him reach for his second gun. "Ned Shute?"

"Ned Shute?" Another voice, softer and sweeter in tone came from his left. "He ain't alone, boss?"

"Who the blazes are you?" Matt felt the pain shoot up from his twisted ankle to his knee.

"Shut him up, Hog," the first of the two voices, the growler, yelled.

Matt's finger squeezed on the trigger, but before he could fire, a rough-spun rope tightened around his neck from the back. He turned to look, but something hard hit him on the head.

Seeing a haze of red and white before his eyes, he tried to swing around to face his attacker, but his knees wobbled, and he went down. The dimness around him got even darker, and the sweet sound of feminine laughter was the last thing he heard before everything went black.

CHAPTER 10

att woke up to the sound of horse hooves cantering up toward him. He sat up quickly and fell back down on his back again, his head spinning fast. It was still dark so must be late at night.

Music from one of the saloons reached his hearing. He sat up again, much slower this time.

"Hey, mister." A youthful voice sounded to his left. "Are you okay?" The boy was young, probably twelve. He sat on a dusky little pony.

Matt peered at the little rider in the dim light. "I reckon I will be…" Matt tried to get to his feet. His sore ankle still hurt. "Once I find out who ambushed me."

"You was robbed, mister?" The boy was looking at him warily.

"You're darn right I was robbed, kid." Matt got to his feet and reached for his guns.

He didn't have any, and neither did he have his gun belt. And all his money was gone. He looked in the direction he had his horse hidden. But Dark Lightning too was gone. Seemed like he was robbed of everything.

"You can tell the sheriff…" the young boy said with a fearful look.

"Heard the sheriff's out of town."

"The deputy ain't."

"Who are you, kid? And what're you doin' out here so late?"

"It's five in the morning, mister," the boy replied. "I'm deliverin' the milk, like I always do every mornin'."

"Oh, then you'd best be on your way, junior." Matt spat, his head beginning to throb where he was hit. "I wouldn't want to hold you up from makin' them deliveries."

"You'd best get to the sheriff, mister," the boy said before urging his pony on.

"I'll do that, after I settle things with an old friend at the saloon." Matt growled and dusted himself off. At least he wasn't robbed of his clothes and boots.

He picked up his hat from the gravel and dusted it before placing it back on his head. Dark Lightning was nowhere near where he had left him.

Matt cursed himself for not setting the gelding up at the stable near the saloon. His ankle still hurt, but he put it past him and began the slow walk back down toward Fat Farley's Saloon.

The first pale rays of dawn were breaking across the dark sky by the time Matt hobbled up to the saloon. He pushed the swinging doors open slowly and stepped inside. The place was not as full as the night before, just a few drunks sleeping off the booze wherever they had fallen over during the night.

He stepped in behind the vacant bar counter and grabbed a bottle of whiskey. Licking his parched lips, Matt undid the cap and drained the bottle in one long gulp. He flung the bottle across the bar, smashing it against the far wall. He waited a moment before hurling the shot glasses one by one and creating a racket early in the morning.

"What in thunderation…" He heard the skinny bartender's voice as the man came running down from upstairs.

The man was in his pajamas, holding a crowbar in his bony hands. His eyes bugged at the sight of Matt sitting on top of the counter with a half-finished bottle of bourbon in his hand.

"Your friends should've killed me, pardner," Matt said in a low growl. "Instead of just robbin' me."

"What the sam hill are you…" the man railed and came at him with the crowbar raised above his balding head.

"Ah, that selective loss of memory you're sufferin' from." Matt laughed sardonically and flung the half-full bottle at the man. "Let me fix that for you."

The bottle hit the onrushing man right in the face, making him drop the crowbar and fall in a crumpling heap. Matt was on him before the man could hit the wooded floor of the saloon.

A right and a left jab made whatever teeth the man had left come flying out of his wide-open mouth. Matt raised his hands high to deliver a two-fisted finishing blow to the skinny man's head when he felt something cold touch the back of his neck.

"That'll be enough, boy." The calm voice of a seasoned lawman echoed behind him. "Now get off Farley, or I'll be forced to put a hole in your head."

"I'm givin' him what he's owed," Matt growled, not looking back.

"The hell you are." A strong hand grabbed him by the collar and pulled him off the semi-conscious bartender and hurled him half across the room.

Matt sat up quickly and shook his head. He looked up at the man standing before him. He was tall and big, dressed in clean clothing suited to a city slicker.

The man's eyes were hard and sharp, even though he looked near sixty. His silver white hair and beard told of his experience and the gold star badge gave him the authority to exercise that experience.

"Who the sam hill are you, feller," the man asked him in that calm yet assertive tone he used the first time, "to think you can come into my town and rough up upstanding citizens under my protection?"

"This snake is anything but upstanding." Matt glared at the man addressing him. "He got me robbed..."

"Robbed? Can you prove that?"

"He told me Ned Shute was fixin' to rob the bank... that he was lookin' for men to join him on that heist."

"And who in the blazes is Ned Shute?" The older man raised an eyebrow.

"An outlaw... a man I am lookin' for..." Matt blinked his eyes. His head still throbbed from the blow he got the night before.

"So, you were aimin' to rob the bank with this Shute feller?"

"No." Matt shook his head slowly. "I was only looking for him."

"Why?"

"To return a favor."

"Then you're his friend." The older man narrowed his steel gray eyes. "That would make you an outlaw too."

"Listen, deputy..." Matt raised his hand in deference. "There's been a mistake."

"Deputy? I am the sheriff of this here fair town of Willow Springs." The silver-haired man stood up straight. "There's been a mistake all right, and you made it... coming here to my town to disturb the peace."

"No... I... I was askin' about Ned Shute to the bartender..." Matt could sense that this man meant business. "He sent me off to get robbed by his associates..."

"And why should I take your word over Farley's?"

"Cause he's a liar." Matt was getting really exasperated. "He told me the sheriff... that is you, were out of town... He lied..."

"As a matter of fact, I was out of town," the sheriff replied calmly. "Just got back early in the morning... to find this ruckus goin' on here at Fat Farley's."

"He set me up to get robbed." Matt almost howled. "I paid him near three dollars for information on Ned Shute…"

"You can't prove any of that," the sheriff told him. "And I seen with my own eyes that you beat an upstanding man near to death… That's aggravated assault, young feller… You get six to nine months in jail for that in this here town."

"You're goin' to lock me up?" Matt couldn't believe what he was hearing. "After *I* get robbed?"

"You're goin' on trial before the judge later today… Till then, you're welcome to stay at the holdin' cell in my office."

"You've got to be kiddin' me." Matt burst out in rage. "I'm lookin' for my brother's killer… and you're…"

"Hold on now…" The older man eyed him with keen interest. "Your brother's killer?"

"This Ned Shute… he was in Cripple Creek, he killed my younger brother, Tommy…"

"And you're chasin' the man to even the score?"

"I aim to send him to hell…" Matt clenched his jaw.

"And what does the sheriff of Cripple Creek have to say?"

"He doesn't know I am doing this."

"Well, then…" The sheriff of Willow Springs placed his hands on his hips. "That plumb near makes you an outlaw. You aim to take the law in your own hands, and that… we law-abidin' citizens can't allow."

"But you don't understand…" Matt felt desperate. "I've been trackin' the coyote for weeks… I know he's here… Help me bring him to justice then, Sheriff."

"Tell me more about this Shute feller."

"I'll do one better… I'll show you…" Matt said and reached for his holster belt, only to realize his money belt along with the wanted poster of Ned Shute was not on him.

"Well?" The sheriff gave him an impatient look.

"I would've… shown you…" Matt gritted his teeth. "But I was

robbed of everything I had on me, exceptin' for my clothes and boots."

"Then you have no proof for anythin' you said so far," the sheriff drawled. "And all I can see you as is a vagrant, a drifter who wandered into my town, drank free whiskey here at Fat Farley's Saloon, and beat the owner near to death. You'll be lucky to get six months from Judge Murdock. Up to me, I'd lock you up for twelve."

CHAPTER 11

The loud clang of a shotgun butt being smashed against the iron bars made Matt glare anew at the lanky deputy on the other side. Almost twenty-four hours had gone by since he'd been thrown in the holding cell of the sheriff's office.

No money, no guns, no food, no horse, and now no freedom.

"I've got to get the hell out of here," he cried out in frustration.

"Oh, you will, pardner," the deputy drawled as he drank coffee from a tin cup. "You'll be out of here in no time, headed right for the proper jail in Santa Fe."

"That's real funny, slim." Matt ground his teeth. "Maybe you should join the theater company."

"We ain't had a troublemaker like you in Willow Springs for a while now." The deputy laughed. "You sure made the day interestin'."

"Why don't you let me out, slim?" Matt grabbed a hold of the iron bars and rattled them. "I reckon I can make things even more interestin'…"

"Oh, no. Not me." The blond man wearing the deputy sheriff badge shook his narrow head. "I won't have Sheriff Cole trading me for you in that there jail."

"Ever been an outlaw, slim?" Matt goaded the young man. "You never lived if you haven't. No laws, no rules… freedom of every kind."

"Except when you get strung up, kid." Sheriff Cole walked into his office and took his seat. "That's how an outlaw's excitin' life always goes down, swingin' from one tree or another."

"Sheriff Cole," Matt said, "you've got an innocent man locked up."

"Where?" Cole leaned back on his chair and rested his shiny boots on his desk.

"Don't play dumb with me, Sheriff." Matt rattled the bars. "You know I'm innocent…"

"Save it for the judge at your trial, boy," Cole drawled and lit a cigar. "I ain't the one who you can plead to."

"Who's the judge?"

"John A. K. Murdock," Cole answered with a snort. "And he don't take kindly to vagrants vandalizing establishments and beating down honest citizens."

"That walkin' corpse of a bartender ain't no honest citizen." Matt kicked at the bars. "He lied and set me up to get robbed… He deserved what I gave him, and I'll give him more…"

"Cuff him and get him out of there, Joey," Cole told his deputy. "Judge Murdock's ready."

"Put your hands out through the bars, pardner." Joey Judd, the deputy, grinned at Matt. "You're getting out of here like you wanted."

"Let's get on with it," Cole said and stepped outside onto the porch.

Matt stumbled out, his hands cuffed and feet hobbled. Deputy Judd prodded him in the back with a shotgun, urging him onward. The midday sun made his eyes water, being locked indoors in the dimness for an entire day.

The courthouse was a short walk away, and a small affair it was. Just a few chairs and benches, and court was already in session with a stern-looking, bald, heavyset man seated in the judgment seat on the high platform.

A ragged-looking man was being led down from the defendant's stand and ushered out in cuffs. Matt found himself being shoved in to take his vacated spot. The baggy-eyed judge looked him up and down and rapped his mallet for silence.

Two men walked in, helping a very battered Horace "Fat" Farley onto the plaintiff's chair. The hatchet-faced bartender gave Matt a very sour look.

"For the charge of assault and battery, damage to private property, and willful disturbance of the peace brought forth by the plaintiff Horace Farley, and seconded by Sheriff Morgan Edson Cole, how does the accused... er, what's his name? Ah, here it is... the accused Matt Dawson plead?"

"He's a darn liar and a thief. He set me up..." Matt yelled, waving his cuffed hands before him.

"Guilty or not guilty?" The judge overrode Matt's outburst.

"But I... they robbed me... all my money... my guns... my horse..."

"Now you listen, young man, and you listen well." Judge Murdock rapped his mallet on the desk. "You answer to only what you are being asked. Any more yelling from you and I will have the sheriff lock you up without trial for a year. Do you understand me?"

"I... um... yes, sir. I do."

"Very well. How do you plead?"

"Not guilty, sir."

"The correct term to address a judge is your honor..." Murdock cleared his throat. "But I'm not going to nitpick on that. Now do you need a defense attorney?"

"I... no." Matt exhaled deeply. "I can't afford one now... I'll defend myself."

"The territory can provide you with a defense counsel."

"Much obliged, your honor, but I can defend myself."

"As you please." Judge Murdock nodded and turned to the prosecution. "You may present your case."

A slender man in a dark city-slick tan suit and black hair combed down flat against his skull stepped up and smiled at the judge and around the small room. "Your honor and respected members of the town council, on the morning of the sixth of this month, my client, the very respected citizen and business owner, Mister Horace F. Farley was brutally attacked, and his establishment vandalized by the accused Matt Dawson who stands before you there."

A buzz spread around the room: of hushed voices, loud indignant voices, and soft whispered voices. Judge Murdock's mallet rose and fell three times, demanding silence.

"Could you tell the court what happened, Mister Farley?" The gaunt prosecutor gestured at his haggard client.

Hatchet-faced Horace "Fat" Farley made as if to speak and went into a bout of coughing. Matt glared at the bartender, disgusted by the obvious playacting.

After a sip of water, Farley looked up pleadingly at the judge. "It was early in the morning, your honor," he began painfully. "I heard a loud crash downstairs in the bar. So I ran down... expectin' the usual drunks to be fightin' and reckoned I'd just chase them out as always... but I was plumb wrong. This feller here, I never saw ever before, was breakin' all my whiskey bottles and glasses, throwin' 'em willy-nilly all over my nice and clean establishment."

He paused for effect, looked around the room, and took another sip of water. "And then... when I asked him gentleman-like who he is and why he's makin' a ruckus... this madman, he just jumped me... and hit me on the head with my own bottle of whiskey. He broke all my teeth, your honor... and I reckon he was fixin' to kill me if not for our Sheriff Cole comin' in time to save my life."

"Is that all, Mister Farley?" his attorney asked, and the

bartender nodded his balding head.

"You may step down, Mister Farley," the judge said and looked at the prosecutor. "Call your first witness, Mister Merrill."

"Thank you, your honor." Merrill had a smirk on his thin lips, making his slender moustache twitch. "I call upon Sheriff Morgan Edson Cole to the stand as my first witness."

"I swear to tell the truth, the whole truth…" the sheriff droned the oath as Matt let his mind wander, cursing himself for getting into this farce of a trial. He should've known better than to trust a bartender in a strange town, especially one who so readily let his jaw wobble for a few cents.

Was he in trouble? It sure looked like he was. It was plain to see all these folks were in cahoots and there was little chance for him getting out of there too soon. He hoped this Judge Murdock would listen to his side of the story and make an honest and just call.

"What did you see, Sheriff Cole?" The prosecutor's piercing voice sliced into Matt's thoughts, and he turned his attention back to the kangaroo court that was being played out before him.

"I just rode into town, after sortin' the mess on the Santa Fe Trail, and as I went past Fat Farley's, I heard bottles bein' smashed. I figured the same as Farley, probably drunks raisin' bob that I may need to break up." Cole paused and looked around the room for effect. "So I walk in and what do I see? Farley almost gettin' skinned alive by this vagrant drifter covered in trail dust. So, I cuffed him and now he's here bein' judged."

"I commend you, Sheriff, on a job well done." Merrill the prosecutor gestured at the sheriff to step down. "You may return to your seat."

"That's my job, mister prosecutor." Cole was grinning wide. "To uphold the law in this here town of mine."

"And now I call on the defendant to… defend himself." Merrill gave Matt a dirty look.

"You may stand and proceed, Mister Dawson." Judge Murdock rapped his mallet on the desk.

"I'll have to start at the beginnin'… your honor," Matt began.

"You'll have to keep it short and quick." Murdock looked at his pocket watch. "We'll be going to recess in a half hour."

"I'll be done well before that, your jud—your honor." Matt nodded his head. "I came here to Willow Springs, New Mexico, lookin' for a man… a wanted outlaw… who committed a crime in Cripple Creek, the town where I come from. I've been trackin' this coyote for two weeks now, and his trail led to here. His name is Ned Shute… a name that no one here has ever heard of. I had a picture of him on a wanted poster, but that was stolen from me.

"Now I walked into Fat Farley's Saloon the day I rode into town and had a conversation with the bartender… at that time I didn't know his name or that he owned the place. A conversation that cost me three dollars and some. Mister Farley here said to me that he knew Ned Shute by lookin' at the wanted poster I showed him, and he told me Shute was fixin' to rob the bank. He even drew me a map where I could find Shute down by the blacksmith's near the southern gate.

"I went there at the stroke of nine and met a feller, who then led me into an ambush and robbed me of everything I have, exceptin' for my clothes and boots. I knew then, when I came to, that I was set up to be robbed by this very upstanding citizen of your town here. So, I took it upon myself to get some retribution from Fat Farley."

"A very interesting story, young man," Merrill said as he walked up to Matt. "But that's what it is, a story… unless you have any proof for all your claims."

"I was robbed…" Matt replied coldly. "Anythin' I could use as proof was taken from me."

"I see." Merrill turned to the judge. "I have no further questions, your honor."

"Very well, Mister Merrill," Murdock replied and turned to

look at Matt. "Do you have any witnesses to support your story, Dawson?"

"Well, I would," Matt said with scorn, "if this whole darn town wasn't against me."

"It isn't like that, Mister Dawson." Murdock rapped on his desk. "This is a court of law, and all claims must be substantiated with proof."

"Well, I reckon I could ask the two ladies who were present when I first conversed with Farley," Matt said with a deep sigh.

"Do you know their names?" The judge narrowed his eyes at Matt.

"Miss Lilly and Miss Molly..." Matt shook his head, acknowledging the futility of it. "But these lovely ladies are employed by Mr. Farley here, so I wouldn't expect anythin' less of them than bein' loyal to the man who pays them."

"Are you insinuating that they would not be trustworthy as witnesses?"

"No, your honor..." Matt shrugged. "I'm sayin' they would have no reason to take the side of an unknown stranger against someone who they know and work for."

"Do you have any other witness, Mister Dawson?"

"I don't reckon I do... your honor."

"Then I will pass judgment based on what has been presented before me in all fairness." Judge Murdock rapped his mallet on the desk again. "Matt Dawson, I find you guilty on all charges pressed by the plaintiff and hereby sentence you to nine months of hard labor in the Santa Fe County jail, unless you pay a bail amount of five hundred dollars."

"Your judgment is solely based upon their word against mine," Matt challenged the judge.

"Yes." Murdock gave him a cloudy look. "I happen to know them a whole lifetime longer than I know you... and vagrant vandals like you move in and out of towns looking for a hog-killin' time at the expense of decent hard-workin' citizens. You deserve your sentence, Matt Dawson of Cripple Creek."

"I can tell you with certainty, Judge Murdock," Matt responded with vehemence, "that I ain't no vagrant, and no drifter neither..."

"Court is adjourned." Murdock hammered his mallet hard on the desk. "Take him away, Sheriff."

"Tell me, Judge..." Matt called out even as Sherriff Cole grabbed him by the collar. "You have heard of the Woodrow Dawson ranch of Cripple Creek, Colorado."

Murdock paused for a moment. "Yes, I reckon I have."

"I stand to inherit that property in time, Judge."

"You... you're Garrett Dawson's son?"

"Yes." Matt nodded. "And Garrett Dawson raised no drifter or vagrant."

"Why should I believe you?"

"Because my father can pay the bail amount of five hundred for my release in a heartbeat."

"Cripple Creek is more'n fifteen days of hard ridin' away." Sheriff Cole spoke up. "It'll take a whole month to get that bail money here."

"Let me take out a loan from your town bank to pay the bail and then have the bank settle this with the Cripple Creek bank."

"This sounds good, but only for you." Murdock's baggy eyes twitched. "For if the Cripple Creek bank refuses the transfer, you get away scot-free and we get nothing."

"That's not goin' to happen." Cole laughed. "We'll keep you here in a warm cozy jail cell, Dawson... for as long as it takes for the bail to get here. And if you're a good little varmint, we might gift you a horse and a gun when you leave."

"I reckon that's the best deal I can get then." Matt exhaled heavily.

"I reckon you reckon right, pardner." Deputy Judd laughed

and prodded Matt in the back with his shotgun to get him moving.

CHAPTER 12

"So that's how it's goin' down then." Deputy Judd grinned at Matt from the other side of the iron bars of his holding cell. "I reckon I'll be ridin' off to see your pa and get the bail money from him."

"I reckon that could happen, Deputy," Matt said somberly and slid down onto the hay-covered wood floor. "Or somethin' else could happen too."

"Like what?" the deputy asked as he slid a plate of bacon and beans into the cell.

"A couple of things…" Matt replied with a sigh and picked up the plate of cold food.

"You mean your pa can chase me away without the bail money?"

"He could do a lot worse." Matt took a whiff at the stale meal and put the plate back down on the floor with disgust. "Pork and beans every day, three times a day… ain't you folks here got any beef… corned beef and cabbage maybe?"

"Beef's too expensive to waste on drifters and polecats…" The deputy grinned with malice. "Now elaborate, boy… What're the worst things your old man could do?"

"He could have you filled full of lead plumbs for one." Matt shrugged. "Or just lock you up in one of the many barns on the ranch…"

"He wouldn't dare… I am a man of the law."

"Not Cripple Creek law…" Matt laughed. "There you'd just be another man askin' for ransom money like a goldarn kidnapper."

"Could that really happen?" The slender deputy's eyes went wide.

"You don't know my pa, deputy." Matt smiled coldly. "You'd best be askin' a bull to a dance than askin' my pa for ransom."

"But I got to do this…" Deputy Joey Judd sounded quite anxious. "Sheriff Cole and the judge ordered me…"

"I got an easy way out for you, pardner."

"What way?"

"You take me with you… hand me over for the bail money and get back here."

"I can't let you out of the cell. Cole will have my hide for that."

"That's the only way we can all come out winnin', Deputy." Matt pushed his untouched plate of food out of the cell.

"Well, I reckon… I could sneak you out in the middle of the night." Joey Judd rubbed his narrow chin. "The sheriff's goin' to be away at Fat Farley's till late."

"His favorite water' hole, I reckon." Matt glared at the picture of the silver-haired sheriff on the wall above the man's chair.

"He does like spendin' his time there aplenty." The deputy nodded. "Been doin' that for years."

"Tonight then…" Matt said, leaning back onto the wall of his cell.

"I'll tell you about it after the evenin' meal," Judd replied and walked out to the porch.

"I hope it ain't stale bacon and beans again." Matt sighed and rested his head on the wall, closing his eyes.

He sat silently for a while, wondering what the night would

bring. Could he trust the deputy? Would the man be greedy enough to take Matt's bait and help him escape?

But more importantly, was Matt ready to take a risk like this? The deputy could easily frame him for trying to escape if the sheriff found out about his little trick. And last he remembered, escaping convicts were almost always shot, even if they surrendered.

A cold draft suddenly blew in from the cracks between the wood planks of the cell wall. It was good to feel the cool breeze on his face, however little there was. Matt was reminded of the open plains of the ranch.

He reminisced about all the times he rode like the wind on his horse, with the breeze blowing on his face and hair. He missed that, feeling suddenly very homesick. Was it worth it? All this trouble he was going through? Would killing Ned Shute make any difference to him and the world at large?

Then Tommy's smiling face floated before his mind's eye, and Matt choked up a sob. He gritted his teeth, reaffirming his resolve to avenge his brother.

He swore anew to himself and to the Almighty, and he prayed for the strength to persevere on his mission. Ned Shute had to pay for what he did. Matt clenched his fists. Even if it took him a lifetime to do it, it was worth it.

CHAPTER 13

It had to be past midnight, Matt figured, when he heard the soft click of the door to the sheriff's office being opened. A slender figure shrouded in shadow crept in and walked up on tiptoe to his holding cell.

The key was turned, and the door opened with a low creaking sound. The deputy pressed the cold barrel of his shotgun against Matt's gut and motioned with a jerk of his head to step outside.

Matt nodded and did as he was ordered. Outside in the dark chill of the night, he saw four horses saddled. Two riders wearing serapes and wide-brim hats sat on two of the horses, waiting for them. He glanced at the deputy.

Joey placed a finger on his lips and gestured at him to mount up. It was a moonless cloudy night, and only the dim light from Fat Farley's Saloon on the far side made it possible to see.

Matt got onto the saddle, his wrists still cuffed, and the deputy grabbed a hold of the reins of his horse and led the party of four out the southern gate of Willow Springs. Matt eyed the shadowy form of the blacksmith's with a grimace as they passed it.

For a few hours, they rode at a slow trot in deathly silence before Deputy Joey kicked his horse into a full gallop at the first sign of a new dawn breaking. Matt found himself being jerked backward hard as his horse took full flight. The four horses thundered down the trail in the rapidly lightening skies as they headed north.

"Two darn weeks before we get there." The deputy finally broke the silence. "And another two to get back."

"We can do it quicker if we lose your two mysterious partners and take the spare horses," Matt called out over the thundering of hooves.

"You're mistaken if you take me for a fool, Dawson." Joey Judd laughed. "Nellie and Shayne are here to make sure you keep up your end of this bargain."

"And what was my end of the bargain?"

"Real cute, pardner." Joey smirked. "Your end is keeping your mouth shut and letting your pa know we have you for real… and the bail money ain't five hundred, but more like a ransom of twenty-five hundred."

"If you think my pa's goin' to let you get away with that—"

"Oh, he will." Judd grinned. "I'll be keepin' my shotgun stuck to the back of your neck the whole time we'll be dealin' with your rich rancher daddy."

"We need to rest the horses," one of the other riders called out to Judd.

"And grab a bite to eat…" the other one, smallest of the four, added. The voice sounded familiar to Matt, even muffled under the dark bandana. He was sure he had heard that high-pitched voice before.

"We find a stream, we rest," Judd told the two of them.

"There's one a mile west of here," the short, high-pitched one said.

"Let's head there then," the deputy replied and urged his horse westward.

The stream was narrow enough to cross on foot. Judd and his

cohorts dismounted and tethered the horses to a tree. Matt found himself dragged off the saddle and dumped onto the ground beside the stream.

A thick strip of jerky was pushed into his mouth, and he chewed on it gratefully. This was the first bite he had since the evening before.

His captors made a small fire and put some beans in the pan. Matt watched them intensely as the two known as Shayne and Nellie discarded their large hats and serapes. He narrowed his eyes.

The larger one was the coyote who had met him that night in front of the blacksmith's. The other one—he stifled a gasp—was a woman. She eyed him with a smug look on her pretty face. It came back to him then: it was her voice he had heard that night, right before he was knocked senseless.

What were his robbers doing with the deputy?

"That's Shayne, and this purty gal here is Nellie." Judd had a sneer on his narrow face. "I believe you met them before."

"They're the ones who robbed me," Matt replied in a flat, emotionless tone. "So, you lawmen of Willow Springs are in cahoots with your outlaws."

"You could reckon we have an arrangement." Judd laughed as they passed the freshly baked beans around. "Works out well for everyone… We all make a fair share, no one gets hurt, and the good people of Willow Springs prosper in peace."

"Is the sheriff the leader of your outfit?"

"Ol' silver hair." The man called Shayne laughed rudely. "He ain't got a clue about any of this."

"Then who's in charge?"

"What're you goin' to do knowin' that pardner?" Judd said as he licked his spoon.

"Is it Shute?"

"Shute?" Nellie asked. "He's asked that before… the night we robbed him."

"Yep, I did." Matt glared at the woman. "Is he the boss…?"

"Who?" Judd looked at him curiously.

"Ned Shute."

"Never heard of…"

"Yep, reckon you haven't." Matt shook his head and sighed.

"All right, we're done restin'" Deputy Judd grabbed a hold of Matt's collar and pulled him up onto his feet. "Mount up, we got a lot of ridin' left to do."

Matt stumbled as he was roughly pushed and made to mount. His captors kicked their horses into a gallop, and they were off again. The dry arid country around them went on for miles.

The noonday sun beat down hard on them, and Matt felt tired and drowsy. He let his mind wander between dreams and daydreams. He wasn't sure whether he had fallen asleep in the saddle, but when he found his focus, he noticed they had stopped again.

It felt too soon since the last stop, and Matt looked around him. He got a start when he noticed the dozen or so riders surrounding him and his three captors.

Deputy Judd had his shotgun against his shoulder, ready to shoot. The other two kept their hands by their sides. The horses nervously fidgeted and whinnied.

Matt scanned the twelve riders forming a semicircle in front of them. Hats low on their brows and eyes cold and hard, these men had the look of hungry wolves cornering a moose.

"Well, looks like we have a standoff," one of the twelve men said in a gruff tone of voice.

"Four to one," another of them added. "Just the odds we prefer."

"More like three to one, I reckon." The first one laughed. "That hombre in the cuffs ain't here on his own accord."

"That's right." Deputy Judd spoke up with a quiver in his voice. "We're on official New Mexico law business… We're transportin' this prisoner to Colorado."

"Prisoner, 'ey?" the gruff one, probably the leader of this gang of twelve, growled. "What's he done?"

"Ain't none of your concern."

"Oh, it is my concern."

"You'd best back off and let us be on our way." Judd trained his gun on the leader.

"Or else what?"

"Or… or…" Judd glanced at his two companions.

"Looks like your friends ain't backin' your claim, lawman." One of the twelve men smirked.

"So now it's twelve against one," the leader said with a snort. "Or more like fifteen to one, seeing neither of your party agree with you."

"There are more men following us… including the sheriff." Judd tried to bluff but failed, making all twelve of the outlaws laugh out loud.

"I'll give you a fair choice, lawman," the leader said slowly. "You lay down your guns and hand over all your money and supplies, and I let you go. Or you die and we take your guns and all your money and supplies."

"How about I keep my guns, money, and supplies…" Judd shook with trepidation. "And put you into the ground?"

"You're a smarter man than that, Deputy." Matt felt like he needed to intervene, sensing an opportunity to escape. "And though I'd like nothin' better'n to see you filled with lead, I reckon you should do as the man says."

"He's got a brain on him, your prisoner." The outlaw leader grinned at the deputy. "And I reckon I could use a man like him in my outfit."

"You can't take a prisoner off a lawman." Judd was clearly shaking. "It would be aidin' and abettin'."

"And who's goin' to put that charge on me?" The leader growled. "A dead lawman?"

"I ain't no lawman." Shayne held up his hands.

"Me neither." Nellie followed Shayne's lead.

"And you ain't no man either, darlin'." The leader looked hard at the woman. "I could use three more grunts in my outfit."

"We'll be much obliged." Matt seized the opportunity.

"Drop your firearm, lawman," the leader told Judd in a cool calm tone. "You're all alone now."

Judd hung his head and lowered his shotgun, much to Matt's relief. Shayne walked over and took the cuffs off him and slapped them on Deputy Judd's slender wrists. The man didn't so much as look up at his former associate.

"Well, now that it's all settled, I'd like to formerly invite y'all to join the Hell Riders gang." The gruff-voiced outlaw leader laughed.

The Hell Riders, Matt laughed softly. He had heard of this band of ruffians. They'd often harass the cattle drives and steal horses, even hold up a stagecoach or two.

He never in his wildest notions thought he'd be joining up with a gang of outlaws like the Hell Riders. At the first chance he would get, Matt decided, he'd break away and put as much distance between him and this predicament he was forced into.

"You there… prisoner," the leader called out to Matt. "You got a name?"

"Sure, I do."

"Well, spit it out."

"You first?"

"Me first…?" The large man threw back his head and laughed. "I like you, boy… you got a pair of big brass ones."

"This here is Big Bill Branson." One of the Hell Riders edged his horse in closer. "The meanest, most ornery sonova—"

"I heard of Big Bill." Matt nodded. "It's an honor to meet you, Big Bill. My name's Matt."

"Matt." Big Bill nodded. "Well, howdy, Matt. You any good with a shootin' iron?"

"Loan me one and I'll show you." Matt grinned.

"Sure thing, pardner." The Hell Rider who introduced their boss whipped out an old pistol, put one bullet down its muzzle, and tossed it over.

"What's the target?" Matt grabbed the old Derringer and twirled it on his finger.

"Him." Big Bill pointed his gun at Deputy Judd.

"Don't mind if I do." Matt grinned and turned to face the surprised deputy.

"But... but... I'm unarmed..." the lanky blond man babbled, his eyes almost bugging out of his head.

"Can you shoot his hat off his—" Big Bill stopped midsentence; his eyes wide in awe as Judd's white Stetson went flying off his narrow head.

"Wheeooo!" Someone whistled. "Now that's some fancy shootin'."

"Well, I'll be darned." Big Bill looked impressed. "You're near as good as this other feller who joined my outfit a week back."

"Who?" Matt asked the larger man.

"A feller from Wyoming." Big Bill grunted. "Name's Ned Shute."

CHAPTER 14

"Ned Shute," Matt murmured under his breath, glancing at his three former captors.

Neither of them made eye contact with him, and he preferred it that way. It wouldn't go down well with Billy Branson and his Hell Riders to know that Matt was looking for Ned Shute. He would have to keep that to himself and find the right moment to avenge Tommy.

"All right then," Branson growled and kicked his horse into a gallop. "Let's get back on the trail."

"Where are we headin'?" Matt asked as he rode up alongside the large outlaw.

"Wherever I say so, pardner." Branson grinned at him. "You're a Hell Rider now, boy… You do as I say, no questions asked."

"You got that, boss." Matt tipped his hat.

"I like you, kid." The large outlaw's grin widened. "And I like your shootin'. We're ridin' for Texas… They got some mighty nice steeds there waitin' for us to bring home."

"Sounds good to me, boss." Matt grinned and pulled back on his horse to let the outlaw leader ride on ahead.

Texas was a good fifteen days' ride further south. Matt

learned Ned Shute was sent there with the advance scouting team. It would take near to a month to get there, he felt sure, for he overheard smidgens of conversation between the Hell Riders about doing a bit of raiding and stagecoach robbing along the way.

About three hours of hard riding later, the group of sixteen riders stopped to rest the horses and fill their growling bellies. Beef jerky and fresh baked beans were passed around as Matt sat himself down by the little stream flowing south.

Deputy Judd had the look of a condemned man on his narrow face. Gone was the smug smirk he had earlier.

Matt felt no joy for it, and neither did he feel any pity. Shayne looked no different from before. He was probably as at home with the Hell Riders as he would have been with any other outfit of outlaws. But Nellie was not her usual cheery self.

Matt detected in her large misty eyes a very visible dread of the terror any woman would have in the company of hungry, violent men.

"How're y'all holdin' up?" Matt asked them in low tones. "Now that the shoe is on the other foot?"

Shayne and Nellie looked up at him, but Judd kept his baleful gaze fixed to the plate of food in his slender hands.

"Shayne?" Matt looked at the man who robbed him.

"I'm all right." He shrugged.

"How about you, Miss Nellie?" Matt looked into the young woman's furtive eyes.

"I… I'm just fine," she replied in almost a whisper.

"I reckon you'd fare a lot better here…" Matt whispered, gesturing at the gang of outlaws sitting around them and eating, "if you were to have a man as your… companion."

Nellie eyed Shayne and then returned her gaze to Matt.

"A companion who can protect you from unwanted atten-tion…" Matt continued in low tones, "…if the need ever comes."

Nellie lowered her eyes and bit her lip.

"Is he that companion?" Matt looked at Shayne.

Shayne cleared his throat and looked away. Nellie kept staring at her booted feet.

"I've got a proposition for you, Miss Nellie," Matt whispered. "I reckon if they—our new friends—think you and I are companions... that might give them the motivation to leave you be, if they were ever plannin' on..."

"He's right, Nellie." Judd suddenly spoke up. "He's earned Billy Branson's respect... None of them will bother you if you and he..."

"Pretend to be companions," Matt finished for the forlorn deputy.

He smiled at the way Nellie's eyes lit up, and he swore he noticed the hint of a blush on her dirt-stained cheeks. This was easier than he had anticipated. Shayne too had a look of relief on his angular face, and Matt gave the man a wide toothy grin.

"I noticed, Shayne..." Matt said, still grinning, "that you're wearin' my gun belt with my Colt Peacemakers still holstered."

Shayne stiffened and eyed Nellie. She pursed her lips and tilted her head toward Matt, urging her partner in crime to do what was right.

"Much obliged." Matt nodded as Shayne undid the gun belt and handed it to him. "And would you happen to have my money on you too?"

His two robbers shook their heads and looked at Judd. The deputy had returned to staring at the ground under his feet. Neither of them would be carrying the money they stole from him on them, Matt knew that, but it felt good to watch them squirm.

"Ah, it's all right." Matt smiled at them. "I reckon you put that money to better use than I would have. I sure wish I still had my horse though."

"Your horse is stabled at the livery in town," Shayne replied.

"I reckon I'll never see Dark Lightnin' again." Matt shook his head sadly. "It'll be a while before I can go back to Willow Springs. And it might be the same for you."

"We could… leave…" Nellie began with a furtive glance over her shoulder.

"And end up with lead plumbs in our backs." Matt gave her a wry smile. "Best ride with them for a while…"

"Until you find this Shute feller you keep askin' for." The pretty woman returned his smile.

"I reckon you might be right there." Matt tipped his hat to her. "Best keep that fact between us too."

"All right, you sorry lot of scalawags, siesta's over." Big Billy Branson's roar startled the horses. "Pull up your britches and get on your saddles. Let's get to ridin'."

Matt watched the twelve Hell Riders mount up and file out the shaded grove by the little stream then leaped onto his saddle and rode out leisurely behind them. He glanced over his shoulder to notice Nellie slowly nudging her gray gelding to ease up right beside him. He gave her a warm smile, which she returned with as much fervor.

CHAPTER 15

Seven days, Matt counted. Seven days the Hell Riders had been on the trail to Texas. The leisurely pace at which they rode made him feel certain it would take more than two months to reach the Lone Star State, especially when Branson and his men planned on making a detour to a nearby town to rob the place. He didn't have to wait long for that to come to pass.

"Hey, kid." One of the Hell Riders rode up on a white mare to where he sat with Nellie and Shayne by an abandoned water mill. "The boss wants you on this raid."

"Just me?" Matt gestured at himself and his two companions.

"Yep." The outlaw nodded. "He wants you to earn your place here among us."

"Fine by me," he replied. "But my lady friend here rides with me."

"She good with a shootin' iron like yourself, pardner?" The man eyed Nellie curiously.

"Nope, but she's gettin' there." Matt gave him a smile.

"Don't reckon the boss is goin' to like that." The outlaw shook his head and looked away.

"Oh, I reckon he'll like it just fine." Matt grinned and stood up. "When are we ridin'?"

"Right now." The man reined his horse around and urged it into a canter. "Com'n."

"You done this before?" Matt whispered to Nellie as they mounted their horses.

She shook her head and stared at him wide eyed.

"Me neither." He smiled and eased his horse onward. "It should be fun."

"What about him?" Nellie gestured at Shayne.

"You reckon he needs me to protect him too?" Matt gave the slender robber a wink.

"No, I mean…" She pushed a lock of hair away from over her eyes.

"He'll be fine here." Matt said as he nudged his horse into a trot. "He's a big bad outlaw, ain't he?"

"No, not really." Shayne shook his head. "You were our first job."

"What in tarnation?" Matt shook his head and patted his horse's neck, making it begin to canter. "I was robbed by a pair of greenhorns?"

"You made it really easy for us." Nellie gave him a smile as she rode up alongside him.

"I reckon I was too eager to get on with my mission." He smiled back at her.

"And now you're not?" She narrowed her eyes at him.

"I have little choice now." Matt shrugged. "At least I'm in the same outfit with Shute… and I can finally get the sonova…"

"What's he done, this Shute feller?" she asked him, her tone of voice as innocent as a child's.

"He's done me wrong, Nellie." Matt sighed. "And I aim to make it right."

"It's personal-like," she prodded.

"Very personal," he said with a tight smile.

"You're a good man, Matt." She smiled warmly.

"Why thank you, Miss Nellie." He tipped his hat.

"Oh no." She shook her head. "Thank you… for keepin' me so well protected in this gang of wild-eyed coyotes."

"Anyone bother you yet…?" He raised his brow questioningly.

"Nary a one of 'em," she replied with a blush. "I overheard some of them sayin' you're the fastest gun they ever saw."

"Yep, they better believe it…" He nodded with grin. "And they better not bother the fastest gun's lady."

"Do you reckon they really believe I'm your lady?"

"They ain't bothered you yet, you did say."

"Not yet… but they might," she replied almost breathlessly. "And you know that too. That's why you're takin' me with you on this here raid."

"Yep. I don't trust any of these coyotes yet…" Matt replied. "And I never ever will."

"I reckon they may need a little more believin."

"Meanin'?" He raised an eyebrow.

"We could put on a little show for them some time…" she said in hushed tones. "We could hold hands sometimes, maybe even steal a kiss."

"You're a lovely gal and all, Miss Nellie," Matt whispered, "but this is all just pretendin'… And besides, I got a gal back home waitin' for me."

"She sure is one lucky gal." Nellie laughed softly. "But if it's all just pretendin', like you say… it wouldn't hurt her none if she didn't know."

"I'd know, Nellie…" Matt replied somberly. "I—"

"Haulloa!" Branson's earsplitting yell made their horses twitch and whinny. "There you are new guy. Come on, ride up here, before we all get any longer in the tooth."

"Where are we headin'?" Matt kicked his horse into a gallop to ride alongside the outlaw leader.

"A small town, another mile west." Branson grinned, showing

tobacco-stained teeth. "We do the usual emptyin' of the cash registers of all the saloons and shops there."

"And their bank?"

"We hit that too, if they have one." Billy Branson laughed out loud. "I love the way your mind works, kid. You're goin' to do just fine with the Hell Riders."

CHAPTER 16

$\mathcal{M}$att adjusted the bandana over his nose and pulled his Stetson low over his eyes. The seven other Hell Riders with him were equally masked as they rode up toward the small town.

The locals were caught by surprise as the gang turned the corner and thundered toward the town square, firing their guns in the air.

"You and you." Branson pointed with his shotgun at two of his riders. "Take the supply stores, empty out all of the money and all the ammunition."

The two men rode off, even as the outlaw leader instructed the next two to do the same at the post office and the blacksmiths. Then he turned to Matt and Nellie and gestured at the only saloon in town.

"Come with me, you lovebirds." Branson's eyes gleamed. "We're goin' to get a drink."

Dismounting at the swinging doors of the smallish saloon, Branson led Matt and Nellie into the establishment, firing a warning shot into the air. The few people in there already had their hands raised above their heads.

The large outlaw waved his shotgun at the bartender and then pointed it at the cash register.

"Empty 'er out," he growled at the terrified old man and then looked around at the other people there. "Everybody stay where you are. Don't nobody get any funny ideas, don't nobody get hurt."

Matt moved in behind Branson, a Colt Peacemaker in each hand, covering the larger man's back. He nodded at Nellie to keep an eye on the swinging doors.

It didn't look like any of the townspeople were up to doing anything to stop them. The cash register was nearly emptied, and Matt wondered what else Branson was looking to rob.

"And those..." Branson barked at the barman, pointing his shotgun at the display of liquor bottles behind the little man. "The good stuff, all of it."

With a large sack full of jingling money slung over his broad shoulder and two bottles of very pricey whiskey in one large hand, Branson fired another shotgun blast into the air before he ran out of the saloon. Matt followed him, and Nellie, stepping out backward, covered their exit.

"We got everythin'." One of the gang rode up to them. "But there's someone shootin' at us from over yonder."

Matt turned his gaze at the direction the shots were being fired from. It looked like it could be the sheriff's office. Why wasn't the man riding out to stop them? he wondered. Was it even the sheriff doing the shooting or one of the deputies?

"It ain't the sheriff," Branson growled. "No respectable lawman's goin' to shoot at raiders so cowardly like..."

"And so plumb off target." One of the outlaws laughed. "He'd be lucky to hit the side of a barn."

"Must be a deputy or someone tryin' to be one," Matt stated and fired a shot in the direction of the shooter.

The shooting stopped.

"Did you hit him?" Nellie asked in surprise.

"I'll be darned if he did. That'll make him the perfect marksman." Branson laughed. "Now come on, let's get the Sam Hill out of this one-horse town."

Matt rode out last, looking back over his shoulder. He wondered if he had really got the shooter, without even seeing where he was. If he did, that would be the luckiest shot he ever fired. He turned around and turned to follow the others, kicking his horse into a full gallop.

Was he an outlaw now, he wondered. He did commit a crime. At least no one got a look at his face. What would his father say? What would Becky say? And that mean ornery leather-faced sheriff of Cripple Creek? It would be best if he didn't tell any of them the whole story, he figured.

CHAPTER 17

The midday sun beat down hard where Matt sat hiding behind the large embankment of rocks. Ten days now since the gang raided the little town on the southern trail to Texas.

Matt looked upward at the lone buzzard circling in the sky, an ominous sign. It told him that death was in the air. Carrion birds had a natural sense at knowing these things.

He returned his gaze to the dusty road that meandered between the two naturally formed walls of sedimentary rocks along the narrow creek. They were about three days' ride away from the Texas border, and this place, Big Billy Branson had told him, was perfect for ambushing a stagecoach heading out of Texas.

Matt was excited—not with joy, but with the sinister thrill that came in anticipation of doing something that was not quite decent. This was his first stagecoach heist; an act he never would have believed he could ever take part in even a month ago.

Next to Matt, gray-haired Willie Bob Tucker crouched behind the five-foot-high boulder. Their vantage point from a rise beside the trial was a good one to ambush anyone riding down the trail from the Texas border a few miles south.

The stagecoach coming down the trial trundled at a steady pace, its team of four horses doing a regular canter. Now would be a good time to ambush the rich folks traveling from one of the big cities in Texas.

To his left, Dead-Eye Dominic stood still and silent as a statue, his rifle propped against his lean shoulder, his cold eyes focused on the approaching stagecoach. Dominic didn't talk much, if at all. He let this long-barreled Sharps rifle do all the talking for him. Matt had yet to see the man miss his mark.

Up on the trail ahead, the tall, broad-shouldered figure of Billy Branson stepped out of the bushes and held up his hand at the approaching carriage. Matt's heartbeat even faster and his eyes went wider still.

The leader of the Hell Riders, the Big Bug himself, stood like a man gone mad in front of the four-horse stagecoach as it barreled down on him. Matt half expected the horses to charge him down and run over him.

His breath quickened as he gingerly touched the mahogany handle of the Colt Peacemaker nestled in the right holster of his gun belt.

"I reckon the boss must have nerves of steel to be doing something plumb loco like that," Matt whispered over his shoulder to Willie Bob.

"The boss does have guts, for sure," the older man replied as he chewed on a wad of tobacco. "But them coaches stop… they always stop."

And stop they did. The driver of the stagecoach reined in the horse team after applying the handbrake. The group of four stallions came to a halt a mere arm's length away from Big Billy Branson. The tall man engaged the driver and the guard in conversation.

Matt was too far to hear any of it, but he could tell the talk was anything but friendly. The guard raised his shotgun, but before he could pull the trigger, his head exploded in a spray of red. Dead-Eye Dominic never missed, Matt acknowledged, as he turned to look in appreciation at the marksman's rifle barrel smoking from the kill shot.

"Wheew!" He whistled. "That was some…"

"Quit jawin' kid," Willie Bob growled. "Let's get down there."

His heart pounding, Matt fell in step behind the older man. He kept his hand on the handle of his holstered Colt, itching to draw it. From the other side of the road, he saw the rest of the gang step into view and join their leader.

Seven of them they were in all, the members Branson needed for this job. Shayne and Nellie were back with the others, another mile up north of the creek.

"Don't shoot," the driver said as he stepped down from the carriage. "I just got passengers… innocent city slickers… heading for the town of Edson's Gulch to join the church."

"No one's innocent." Big Billy Branson's growl never failed to send a chill down Matt's back. The man's tone was colder than death.

"Get 'em out, pardner." Willie Bob waved his short-handled scattergun at the driver. "We'll relieve them of their sins."

Matt watched in awed silence as the driver opened the stagecoach door to let the passengers out. There were four: two men and two women. They stepped out, their faces white with fear.

The first man looked wealthy enough to own a bank or two. The other man could have been a traveling salesman. The women looked like sisters. Young and pretty, dressed as if they'd rather be in church than on a stagecoach.

"Your donation, if you please." Red Hardy, one of the bigger men of the Hell Riders, held open a large sack. "Hurry now."

"This is prepos—" the old banker began to sputter.

"Maybe you'd like a blue whistler between your beady eyes instead, 'ey?" Branson drew his Colt Single Action Army revolver and jabbed the cold barrel on the startled banker's brow.

"Once we get to Edson's Gu—"

Blam!

The fat old man went down midsentence, his mouth open and round face frozen in indignation. Matt felt his heart leap against his chest. The man was a darn fool to call Big Billy Branson's bluff.

"You soft city folks want what he got?" Willie Bob snarled at the shocked driver and his passengers. "We're gettin' the gold off you either way."

"No." The second man held up his hands. "I'll do what you say… if you let me go."

"Your watch, money belt, and silver buckle first." Red Hardy grinned at the trembling man. "And you too, ladies."

"I have a hankerin' to know more." Branson turned to the man as he emptied his money belt. "You work for the bank… The silver buckle has the bank's marking on it."

"I don't know what…" the man began and stopped when the outlaw leader's smoking gun pointed at his ashen face. "I… please don't shoot… I'll tell you…"

"Much obliged." Branson grinned, the sharp points of his canine teeth gleaming.

"This Friday… the bank's sending the payroll for the railroad…" The man trembled.

"How much?"

"I… I…"

Branson cocked his gun, making the bank employee's eyes bulge even bigger.

"Twelve thousand dollars… in bank notes and gold coins," the man replied, his eyes closing in dreaded anticipation of being shot.

"And the money coach is runnin' down this trail?" Willie Bob looked at the stagecoach driver.

"Yes, yes…" The driver nodded, his eyes widening with dread. "But there'll be more guards…"

"Oh, don't you worry about that, pardner." Willie Bob grinned and kicked at the fallen guard by the carriage wheel. "We know how to take care of guards."

"Now get on your way to Edson's Gulch," Branson barked. "Before I change my mind and bury you all."

Matt watched as the passengers hurried back onto the stagecoach and it rolled away up the trail, resuming the journey to its destination. They left behind the bodies of the two dead men. Branson insisted the carrion birds get their dinner.

"Are you fixin' to leave these poor bastards lyin' here to rot away?" Matt couldn't help asking the outlaw boss.

"If you don't mind diggin' up a couple graves in the hot sun…" Willie Bob gave him a wide grin. "You can go ahead by your lonesome and give them a burial."

"I ain't fixin' to do no such thing." Matt grinned back.

"Haul the bodies behind some of these rocks. Get them off the trail," Branson said and mounted his horse. "We'll be camping in these here parts till Friday."

"So, we're robbing the money coach next…?" Matt rubbed his chin.

"You catch on quick, kid." Willie Bob laughed. "Now come on, give us a hand with these city slickers."

Friday was four days away. That was another four days added to getting to Texas. Almost three months now since Matt had begun his hunt for Ned Shute. Three months since Tommy was killed. He took a deep breath and walked over to help with the corpses.

CHAPTER 18

Friday took long enough to come for Matt. But when it did, he wished it hadn't. The gang was going to hit the stagecoach carrying the railroad payroll in full force. That included all its present members, old and new.

The rest of the Hell Riders and Nellie had joined them in the valley two days ago, and Matt noted Deputy Judd was conspicuously missing. He soon learned the man had attempted to escape, taking advantage of Big Billy's absence, and was shot dead in the process.

Matt didn't know the man well enough to care for the loss either way. But a life lost was a life lost, and not acknowledging it would be rather uncivilized of him. He offered a silent prayer to the Lord for Joey Judd to find forgiveness and peace.

It was almost high noon when Matt heard horses galloping in the distance. He was sitting on a rock inspecting his guns for any little flaws that could make them jam or misfire.

The Colt Peacemakers were in perfect condition. He holstered the guns and stood up just as Billy came walking down the rise he was on.

"Get your sorry hides in position, you sons of coyotes," the large man said in an uncharacteristically low tone of voice. "They're rollin' in fast. At least seven armed guards."

Matt exhaled deeply and took position. The stagecoach came thundering down the trail, accompanied by six riders, two before and four following. They came within a hundred yards of where the outlaws were hiding behind natural formations of rocks and boulders.

"Now!" Branson yelled.

Eight of the gang, four on either side of the trail, stood up to peer over the rock walls and fired their rifles, catching the stagecoach and its escorts in a hail of crossfire. The rifle men ducked down, and the rest of the Hell Riders took their place, firing their pistols.

The horses and the six riders went down. The stagecoach ran over the stumbling and dying horses, pitched sideways, flipped over, and crashed hard onto the ground, trapping the driver and the two shotgun riders under its weighted bulk.

Matt looked away, saddened deeply by the sight of carnage to man and beast alike.

"Move in, boys," Willie Bob yelled as the Hell Riders carefully made their way out of hiding toward the bullet-ridden stagecoach. "Kill anyone of 'em still movin', can't have 'em shootin' at us while we collect."

But the men guarding the stagecoach, all nine of them, were dead, as were the horses they rode and the four that were pulling the stagecoach. Matt felt a hard lump form in his throat. The sight of such magnificent animals, lying dead or dying in pools of red, broke his heart to pieces. And the men, good honest hard-working men who had families back home waiting for them. They would never see home again, nor would their loved ones see them again.

For a moment, Matt felt like turning around and walking away, daring the risk of being shot. But he held back that urge.

He was a man who lost family too. Family so dear to him. Family he would never see again.

He had to do this for Tommy. He exhaled deeply and followed the other outlaws. They were at the stagecoach already, two of them dragging out a large iron-reinforced oak strongbox.

Branson shot the two heavy iron locks off the strongbox and kicked open the lid. He threw back his head and let out a booming laugh. His men joined him.

The strongbox was filled to the top with freshly printed paper bank notes and two heavy pouches made of leather filled with gold coins.

Grim and unimpressed by their deeds, Matt glanced at Shayne. The man appeared to fit right in with the others, laughing and whooping with them. He moved his eyes over to Nellie. She had the same look of concern on her face as Matt had. When their eyes met, she lowered them to her feet.

"We can buy a ranch in Montana now, boys." Branson's loud laughter drowned out the clamor of the carrion birds hovering overhead. "It'll be a mighty fine place for the horses we take from Texas."

"So how soon before we head for them horses?" Matt seized the opportunity as he stepped up beside the outlaw boss.

"Why, we can head on there right now, boy," the large man replied. "Soon as we pack all this up."

"Where are these horses in Texas?" Matt urged.

"A few miles beyond the border, in a valley between two ranches," Branson grinned. "Unbranded wild fillies and mustangs, just waitin' for us to bring 'em home."

"How d'we know if the horses are still there?"

"My cousin Saul and a few of our boys are there, keepin' an eye on things."

"Can they be trusted?" Matt asked, risking the man's ire.

"My own cousin…" Branson furrowed his brow. "Why he'd

have to catch a blue whistler between his teeth if he breaks my trust."

"And the others?"

"The Hoskins brothers? I've known them boys for years…"

"Any of the new guys?" Matt pushed.

"New guys?" Branson scratched his chin. "Yep, there are two. One of them said he was from Wyoming, and he's good at pursuadin' horses to come with him."

"Can you trust these new men?" Matt dared again.

"As much as I trust you, kid." Branson's booming laugh put him at ease a little. "And what's with all these questions…? You're fixin' to be a blood-suckin' lawyer… or worse, you want to write a story in the evenin' newspaper about me?"

"Nope, boss." Matt grinned at the larger man. "I'm just bein' cautious is all."

"Yep, it's all right." Branson brought his large and heavy hand down on Matt's shoulder, making him wince. "We'd best be hastenin' away from here before they send the Texas Rangers down to investigate."

"The Texas Rangers?" Matt asked as he glanced at Nellie.

"Yep. This is a big one." Willie Bob walked past them. "I reckon they'll be lookin' for us in five states for this."

"Are we all goin' into hidin' then?" Matt asked in wonder.

"Hidin'?" Branson laughed. "We never hide. If those ornery lawmen can find us, we'll take the rangers head on. Hell, between Willie Bob, Dead-Eye Dom, and me, we killed more Texas Rangers and U.S. Marshals than I can count on all my fingers and toes."

CHAPTER 19

Despite his boasting, Big Billy Branson and the gang kept a low profile for near on a week after their big heist. The town they were holing up in wasn't much, just a small border post set up to oversee the railroad being built about a mile east.

Branson's instructions were clear. No one was to do anything to draw attention to themselves. They were all just a group of cowboys riding into Texas to look for work wrangling cattle. It was strange to see the rowdy outlaws behave like well-mannered civilized folks for a change.

"You all right, Miss Nellie?" Matt asked the pretty young woman seated beside him at the bar counter of the small saloon. "You been awfully quiet lately."

"I'm all right," she replied, staring at the full glass of cool beer she held in her hands.

"I wouldn't be askin' if you were," he told her, taking a sip of his bourbon.

"All right, Matt," she said softly. "I'm awful skeered."

"Even more'n you've been since we joined up with these pole-cats?" he prodded.

91

"After they killed the deputy…" She took a deep breath. "And the way they slaughtered the stagecoach riders… There's no tellin' when they can do that to me… to us."

"I've been wonderin' that too, Nellie." Matt exhaled heavily. "But I reckon they need us… They need the numbers."

"For how long, Matt?" Nellie sighed. "How long do we have to keep ridin' with them? How long do we have to keep associatin' with all the murderin' they're doin'?"

"Well. I'll be ridin' with them until I get Shute."

"But what if the Rangers get them first?" Nellie stared at him with large, misted eyes. "We'll all hang with them… We'll get charged with the same crimes and murders as them…"

"I don't reckon…"

"And if you find this Shute feller before that… what then? Will you leave me here with these murderin' bastards and ride away into the sunset?"

"No, Nellie… I'll take you with me…"

"Take me where? As what? And why? I only need you here in this pickle to protect me from them. You got a lady at home for you to ride back to… Why would you do anything for me?"

"But Nellie…"

"I never wanted any of this. I never wanted to be in a gang of murderin' outlaws. I was fine bein' a small-time robber, havin' a plumb cozy deal with the law back in Willow Springs. I cuss the day you came ridin' into Willow Springs, Matt. You ruined everythin'… for us… for me."

"Nellie, what's gotten into you?" Matt leaned in closer to her and whispered, "You've not been like this in all these days I've known you."

"It's Joey. They just killed him… in cold blood."

"Who?"

"Joey Judd, the deputy."

"But he was tryin' to escape." Matt gave her a puzzled look. "Clearly against what Branson said."

"You believe them… You believed those murderin' sons of rattlesnakes."

"What really happened, Nellie?" Matt sensed there was more to the deputy's demise than what he was told. "Tell me."

"Joey wasn't tryin' to escape." She wiped a tear away from her eye. "He was… he was defendin' me."

"Uh… what?"

"Yes, Matt… two of them polecats came up to me, wanting what they reckon I've been givin' to you." Her voice trembled. "And owin' that you were away for so long, they said they'd take from me what you weren't there to receive."

"Who are these two bastards?" Matt glanced around the small room.

"Why, Matt? Are you goin' to kill them?" Nellie laughed nervously. "Won't the boss get you for that… and me too?"

"I'll talk to Big Billy. He'll…"

"He'll do nothin' for you, Matt." She almost smirked. "He'll want to back up his own boys… you're just a stowaway in his outfit, someone he can use for a time…"

Matt knew she was right. Branson was using him just as much as he was using Branson to serve his own ends. "Deputy Judd…" He changed the subject. "How did it happen, Nellie?"

"He told them scoundrels to leave me be." She wiped the beer from her lips with the back of her hand. "They laughed at him and came at me, but Joey jumped them so's I could get away."

"Did they…?"

"Yep, they killed him in cold blood." She sighed and looked out the little window. "Joey didn't have a gun… They just shot him, three times."

"You're right, Nellie." Matt nodded grimly. "Branson is not going to do anything about it… and right now I reckon I can't do anything otherwise."

"I know you have your reason to be with them…" Nellie

smiled at him sadly. "But I don't have any. I'm fixin' on running off…"

"What about Shayne?"

"What about him?

"Are you two…"

"He's just as much a stranger to me as you are, Matt," she said. "Fact is I've spent more time talking to you than I ever did with him. I met him a couple of days before we were set to rob you."

"Ah, that reminds me… if it doesn't matter to you anymore." Matt gave her a sheepish smile. "I reckon you could tell me now who was givin' the orders the night I was robbed."

"Yep, it doesn't matter anymore, Matt." She exhaled deeply. "Cause he's dead."

"Dead?"

"Yes, dead as this nail in the wood."

"How did…" Matt scratched his head. "You mean it was… Deputy Judd?"

"Yep, it was."

"And the sheriff?"

"He didn't know a thing." Nellie rolled her eyes. "Just like all the other things Ol' Silver Hair doesn't know about."

"So is Farley the boss of this operation goin' on in Willow Springs?"

"Fat Farley?"

"Yep."

"Nope, he's just another flunky… like us." Nellie shrugged and pushed her half-finished beer away.

"So, then who's the boss?" Matt felt confused.

"I told you," She replied with a sigh.

"Judd?"

"Yep."

"I can't… believe that…" Matt pushed his barstool back and stood up.

"Why not?" Nellie stood up beside him. "Did you know Joey from before?"

"Nope." He shook his head and slapped a few coins on the bar counter for their drinks. "Met him in Willow Springs after that silver-haired sheriff arrested me."

"So, what's not to believe?" Nellie asked as she headed for the saloon doors.

"Well, I reckon…" He followed her outside.

"Joey's dead now," Nellie said as she took a deep breath of the air outside. "And I don't want to be."

"I'll find a way to get you out, Nellie… I promise."

"When?"

"Soon." He tried to smile.

"How soon?"

"In a couple of days."

"If'n we're still breathin' then." She shook her head and walked into the little boarding house for the working women of the railroad she was staying in.

"We will be, Nellie." Matt watched her climb up the stairs to her room. "We will be."

CHAPTER 20

The lush green valley stretched for miles as Matt eased his horse down the sloped grassland. The rest of the Hell Riders were about a quarter mile ahead. He could see them, tiny puffs of brown dust against all the green.

It had been almost four months now since he set off after Ned Shute, his brother's murderer. He was finally going to find that elusive coyote and keep the promise he made to himself on the day of Tommy's funeral.

Up ahead, the gang had brought their horses to a halt and were gathered around in a tight circle. He could hear Big Billy Branson's belligerent voice disrupting the peaceful ambiance of the serene valley, making the horses whinny and stamp as always.

"Where is that goldarn polecat now?" Branson was demanding as Matt rode up to join the crowd.

"He's gone, boss," replied the red-faced man Branson was yelling at.

"Yep, he got on his horse and rode off... to the east," added another man, who resembled the red-faced one.

The Hoskins brothers that Branson had told him about, Matt surmised.

"And you just let him go?" the outlaw boss growled like a hungry grizzly.

"Saul reckoned there was no point chasin' after him." The first brother shrugged.

"And where the blazes is that no-good, bootlickin' cousin of mine?"

"Darned if we know, boss." The other Hoskins shrugged the same as his red-faced brother.

"What's goin' on?" Matt eased his horse in closer.

"The feller from Wyoming messed things up a bit," Willie Bob told him. "He got into a fight at the local saloon, killed the bartender and another fool, then hightailed it out of town."

"When did all this happen?" Matt asked, a tinge of anger flashing across his eyes. He couldn't believe Shute was out of his reach yet again.

"Last week, while we were holed up in that one-horse town by the railroad."

"Are we goin' after him?" Matt looked at Branson.

"He ain't worth it," the outlaw boss snarled. "We got a couple hundred head of fine horses to get... No time for chasin' after deserters."

Matt nodded and eased his horse away from the circle. This was the perfect time for him to take Nellie and make a run for it. Branson and the rest wouldn't even notice. But how and when would he do it?

He'd have to wait for the outlaws to get busy with rustling up all those horses they planned to steal. That could take days, and Shute could be getting further and further away from him.

The murderer was heading east, he heard someone say. How far east and where? Louisiana was east of Texas. Would Shute head for that state or even further east? And what if the coyote made it look like he was heading east, but he rode off in any other direction at any time after that?

Worst of all, the Hoskins brothers could just be plain lying.

Matt took a deep breath and sighed. This was taking way longer than he had naively expected.

The unbranded horses Branson was after were in a valley that was another three-day ride away. Matt knew if he and Nellie didn't ride with the outlaws there, they would be missed, and Branson might then be inclined to come after him.

He would have to wait until the gang was in the thick of rounding up those horses. And that could take near on a whole week.

"I've got to find a better way…" he muttered to himself.

"Better way for what?" Nellie asked him.

He hadn't noticed the woman quietly riding up beside him and was visibly startled by her sudden presence. "It ain't nothin'," he lied.

"You're not as good at lyin' as you are with your shootin'." She laughed softly. "And I know what you're thinkin'."

"What am I thinkin'?"

"The same as me." She smiled and winked. "That now's the time to get away for good from these murderin' rattlesnakes."

"And how'd you figure that?"

"We've been on the trail together for months now, pardner." Nellie smirked. "And even if we're just pretendin' to be… close companions, I've gotten pretty used to the way you do your thinkin' by now."

"Well, I reckon that's a good talent for a smart robber." Matt nodded appreciatively. "And yep, you're right on that count, Miss Nellie. I am considerin' the possibility of doin' just that."

"So, how're we goin' to do this?"

"I'm still workin' on it." He cocked his head. "Have you thought somethin' up?"

"I'm sorta workin' on it too." She gave him a sly smile. "I've got news of somethin' brewin' that might work in favor of us gettin' a way out of this mess."

"You have?" He looked at her with an expression of incredulity on his face. "What is it?"

"We can't talk about it here…" she whispered. "Someone might overhear… and we'd be done for."

"Then where?"

"We can rent a room in town… away from all these murderers. Make it look like lovers needin' some private time before ridin' off to steal horses."

"Er… that might… I don't…" He took a step back.

"That way is the only way, Matt… if'n you're really fixin' to be free of the Hell Riders and goin' after your Shute feller."

"How did you know about Shute bein' gone?"

"You didn't even hear me ride up to you now." She laughed. "You didn't even know when I snuck up on you and clobbered you with a rock that night you were robbed. I know how to move around unnoticed, listenin' for things I'm not meant to."

"I'm wonderin' then if you really needed any protectin' from me."

"Maybe I did, maybe I didn't." She rolled her eyes. "But forget that for now… I really need your help to get out of this mess for good, and you need mine. I'd suggest you do as I tell you. Now let's get us that private time like everyone here expects us lovers to do."

CHAPTER 21

"Here we are now, all alone," Nellie said breathlessly as she closed and locked the door to the little room.

"Er… do we need to lock the door?" Matt stared at the bolted door with some discomfort.

"It has to look real…" she replied. "Those fellers need to know that we really mean business."

"Okay… I reckon you're right," Matt said and leaned against the side wall of the small room they rented on the second floor of the saloon. "Now tell me about the plan you have cookin' for us."

"You want to get right to jawin' about the plan?" Nellie gave him an inviting smile and patted the spot beside her on the small bed. "Don't you want to… have a little fun first?"

"Can't say I don't." He stayed put by the side wall. "But we rented this room for you to tell me about this plan you have."

"Sure, sure," she said with a sigh. "I was hopin' we could have some fun together before we part ways forever."

"Well, I ain't the cheatin' sort, Nellie," Matt replied. "I got a gal waitin' for me back home, and she's the only one for me."

"Ah yeah, that real lucky gal of yours back home." Nellie

sighed and sank down to her elbows on the bed, arching her back. "She must be real purty and decent for you to be so faithful. Or maybe she just has a rich daddy."

"What's this plan of yours, Nellie?" Matt began to feel impatient. "We shouldn't be idlin' away. The sooner we get out of this mess the better."

"At least pour us a drink and sit here on the bed with me."

Matt nodded and poured some bourbon into two small cups, handed her one then sat on the bed at an arm's distance from her.

Nellie downed the drink in one go and snickered at him for sitting away from her. "All right, pardner," she said. "I owe you… for keepin' me safe among those coyotes and, more than that, for not holdin' a grudge against me for robbin' you."

"That's all in the past, best forget about it." Matt sipped his drink slowly. "The future's what we ought to be considerin' now."

"Yep." The young woman sighed. "So, here's what I know is goin' on, and probably so do Big Billy and his coyotes."

"How do I not know about whatever this thing goin' on is?"

"Cause you got your head wrapped up too far in what you want to do, Matt." She laughed softly. "You should keep at least one ear and one eye open to all the other things that're goin' on around you. You'd never ever make a good bounty hunter if you don't look out and listen for things more than you want to."

"I'd reckon you know a lot of bounty hunters."

"Maybe I do, but never you mind that…" Nellie held up her empty cup for a refill. "I heard the Texas Rangers are out in numbers lookin' for the stagecoach robbers from that Friday by Boulder Pass Creek."

"And Branson knew that too. That's why we hid in that little town for a whole week, and then we did most of our ridin' here after dark."

"You'd have figured that out too, if you weren't always thinkin' about gettin' this Shute feller."

"I… you're right, Nellie." Matt exhaled and lowered his head.

"But that darned varmint… he killed my brother, in cold blood… I'll never give up until I put him six feet under."

"From what I heard, this feller's a real cold-eyed killer." Nellie reached out and touched his hand. "Are you sure you're ready to take him on, that is, if you ever find him?"

"I'll find him, Nellie," he replied with conviction. "And may the Lord be my witness, I'll fill him full of lead plumbs."

"You sound purty darn convincin' to me, but before that…" Nellie stared out the little square window of their room. "We've got to get ourselves far away from this gang."

"And you have a plan to do just that, you said."

"Yep. I'm goin' to let the Texas Rangers know where the Hell Riders are."

"How?" Matt eyed her curiously.

"There's a telegraph service in this here town's post office…" she told him. "You'd know about that if you looked around proper."

"But what if Branson and his boys…"

"You got to cover for me when I set out to do that."

"What can I do…?"

"Tell 'em I got womanly stuff I need to see the doctor about." She made a face.

"You reckon they'll buy that?" He rubbed the week-old stubble on his chin.

"If any of them is a doctor, they might not." She smirked.

"When are you intendin' to do this?"

"Tonight, after eight."

"And then what?" Matt stifled a yawn.

"I reckon the rangers can get here by mornin', and we'll be free of those murderin' bastards for good."

"They won't go without a fight."

The more of them that get killed the better." Nellie's eyes blazed.

"What about the Rangers, Nellie? They might reckon us as being with the Hell Riders."

"We'll tell the Rangers the Hell Riders held us as their hostages, Matt." Nellie had a sly smile on her pretty face. "We'll say they forced you to join them on their raids by threatenin' harm to me."

"That's one heckova darin' plan, Nellie," Matt had to admit. "But it sounds crazy enough to work."

"You better believe it will work, Mister Matt Dawson." She gave him a wide-eyed stare. "Now come here and give a girl a little kiss for savin' your life."

CHAPTER 22

*B*ullets whistling past him, Matt kept his head low under the glass windowpane of the post office. The grime-covered glass of the window lay shattered on the ground beside him, shot to pieces in the gunfight that had been raging ever since the Rangers rode into town.

He hadn't expected the Texas law enforcement to get there so quick. They must've already been in and around the area when Nellie sent them the wire. She crouched on the ground behind him, her eyes wide with fear and excitement all at once.

The Rangers came in force right at the break of day, trapping the Hell Riders inside the northern Texan town. Branson and his outlaws were caught unaware but still had managed to hold out against the law enforcers for the last two hours. It was almost noon, and the fighting was still going on.

"How many of us did they get?" Branson yelled out from his hiding place at the bank across the street from the post office.

"Five, from my last count," Willie Bob answered him from his position at the other window of the post office. "Red Hardy and the Hoskins boys among them."

"Are they dead?" Matt whispered over the sound of bullets outside.

"Could be," the outlaw replied. "But I reckon them Rangers took 'em alive."

"How did this happen, Willie Bob?" Nellie asked.

"Someone ratted on us, darlin'." Willie Bob spat out a wad of tobacco. "Once we're through ridding us of them pesky lawmen, the boss is goin' to find out who it was… and have them skinned like a raccoon."

"Do you reckon we can be rid of them?" Matt asked, his guns still holstered. "There's more'n a dozen Rangers out there, and the rest are bounty hunters."

"We've killed plenty of Rangers, marshals, and bounty hunters, boy," the older man snarled. "It's only a matter of time… as long as we stay hidden and don't run out of ammo, we can take out them bastards one at a time."

A loud yell followed by a gurgling sound made them all peer out the windows.

"They got Dead-Eye Dom." Branson's bull voice wafted over from outside. "Goldarn it all."

"Horse feathers!" Willie Bob cursed. "He was our best chance…"

"What do we do now?" Matt asked.

"You can do some o' that fancy shootin' o' yours, pardner, and bag us some Rangers." the grizzled outlaw replied with a growl. "Ain't that why the boss took you in with the Riders?"

"I've never been in a real gunfight like this before," Matt offered with some indifference.

"Is that why you ain't even drawin' your guns, boy?" Willie Bob sneered. "You 'fraid o' the Rangers? You all yeller now?"

"Big Billy Branson!" a loud voice sounded from outside. "You'd best drop your weapons and surrender. If'n you don't, there's no way on the Lord's green Earth you're gettin' out of this alive."

"We Hell Riders'd rather die than surrender, lawman," Branson yelled back.

"And what about the rest of you?" the ranger shouted louder. "You all reckon your boss is worth dyin' for?"

A few more shots followed: the sharp crack of pistols, the blast of a shotgun, and a few reports of rifles being fired.

"And now there's four fewer of you…" the Ranger doing the shouting continued. "And still the twenty-four of us. You all don't have to die, you know… Surrendin' now can get y'all a little more leniency from the judge."

"Darn it all…" Willie Bob gnashed his teeth. "This is it, the Hell Riders' last stand. Come on, you lot, let's get out there, all guns blazin'."

"I ain't that keen to die," Matt said. "I'm much too young for that, and so's my lady."

"If'n you don't go out with us…" Willie Bob aimed his heavy barrel shotgun at Matt. "I'm goin' to kill you and your lady where you stand."

"Matt's right, Willie Bob, we ain't too keen to die neither." One of the younger members aimed his gun at the older outlaw.

"What in thundera—arrrgghh!" Willie Bob fell to his knees, his shotgun flying out of his hands, hands that were ruptured through the palms and bleeding.

Matt had his smoking Peacemakers holstered even before the shotgun hit the ground. "I say we do what the Rangers say, boys." He turned to look at the three other Hell Riders in the post office with them. "You don't want to die for the likes of Willie Bob and Billy Branson."

"I reckon we don't," the oldest of the three said resignedly and dropped his gun belt.

"Hold your fire! Hold your fire!" Matt yelled out to the rangers outside. "We're coming out with our hands up."

"Come out slow and easy," the ranger yelled back. "And keep

your hands where we can see 'em. We got the buildin' surrounded."

"You heard the Ranger, boys." Matt smiled at the three unarmed Hell Riders and the moaning Willie Bob. "Let's get on out there, hands up in the air, nice and high."

The four outlaws filed out of the post office, their faces sullen and eyes low on the ground. Matt followed them out with Nellie behind him.

"This way, gents." The tall Ranger doing all the yelling walked up to them. "On your knees and hands at your back."

"And you there, young feller…" One of the Rangers aimed his rifle at Matt. "You still have your guns on you."

"I reckon he's the one who persuaded these polecats to surrender." The first Ranger walked up to Matt. "And also, who wired the office."

"We did that." Nellie peered from behind Matt's shoulder. "We were bein' held hostage by these murderin' coyotes… for months."

"We'll have to let the judge decide on that… You'll all be goin' on trial," the ranger with the rifle said.

"What in the name of…" Branson yelled from his hiding place in the bank. "You dirty little traitors…"

The large man came running out of his hiding place, guns blazing. Matt grabbed Nellie and dived down onto the ground. Branson was almost upon them, his guns inches away, when both his knees were shattered by rifle bullets.

With a hideous wail, the leader of the Hell Riders went down, his guns slipping out of limp fingers.

"He is the leader of them murderin' coyotes…" Nellie yelled from under Matt.

"Then the rest should give up without much fight, if they have the sense." The first Ranger grabbed Branson by his greasy hair and held his face up. "Round them all up."

CHAPTER 23

After a hot meal of beans, sausages, and bread, Matt was ushered into the sheriff's office of the town. Instead of the sheriff, he found two men who looked his father's age waiting for him.

Nellie was seated there too, across from the two men behind the wide desk made of dark mahogany. One of the men wore a Rangers' uniform and badge.

"My boys tell me you two sent us that wire." The gray-haired, steel-eyed captain of the rangers puffed on his cigar.

"Yes, sir. We did that." Matt tipped his hat.

"And you were held hostage by these sons o' bitches for two months…" The other gray-haired man in the office said, his blue eyes narrowed at Matt and Nellie. "Is that your story?"

"Yep, that's our story, Sheriff." Nellie put on a sweet innocent tone of voice.

"I ain't the Sheriff, darlin'." The man smiled. "But I just might not buy that story."

"Oh, but it's all true…" Nellie made wide doe eyes at the two older men. "Tell them, Matt."

"Yes…" he said haltingly. "That's all… true."

"And you two are together...?" The captain eyed them in turns.

"Yes," Nellie replied.

"No," Matt said at the same instant.

"Yes? No? Which one is it?" The other man raised an eyebrow.

"Well, we had to pretend to be... companions." Nellie shyly twirled a lock of her red hair. "Matt here was purty gentleman-like to protect me from them wild, uncivilized varmints."

"And what were you doin' before the Hell Riders took you hostage?"

"Why we were passengers on a stagecoach they robbed..." Nellie replied hurriedly before Matt could open his mouth. "They robbed us and then took us hostage."

"Where are you from, miss?" the captain asked.

"Oh, I'm from Delaware originally..." Nellie smiled at the man. "But I work in the saloon in Willow Springs, New Mexico."

"We'll arrange for you to return home right away, miss." The captain smiled back.

"So, I don't need to testify or anythin'?" Nellie almost couldn't contain her joy.

"No need for that. We got enough charges of robbery and murder on the Hell Riders to hang them a dozen times over. We can let this kidnapping charge slide."

"Oh, I... I can really go home now," Nellie gushed like a little child in a candy store.

"Sure you can, miss." The captain handed her a piece of paper that he signed. "Here, show this to the Ranger outside, and he'll arrange for you get back home to Willow Springs."

"Oh, I can't thank you enough, Captain." Nellie grabbed the piece of paper and headed for the door. She opened the door and looked back over her shoulder at Matt, blowing him a kiss. "Thank you for everythin' you did for me, Matt. I pray you get home safe too, back to that lucky gal you got waitin' for you."

And with that, she rushed out, slamming the door shut behind her.

"And how about you, pardner?" the man seated next to the ranger captain asked Matt. "What parts do you hail from?"

"I… I'm from Colorado," Matt replied. "And I… I've been on the road for a while… lookin' for someone."

"You look mighty familiar to me, son," the man said. "Take off your hat and lean closer into the light."

"Is he on any wanted posters, Aaron?" the captain asked.

"I don't reckon I've seen him on any, Earl," Aaron replied. "But I know that face… or maybe I'm seein' a ghost."

"He's looks flesh and blood enough to me, Aaron." Captain Earl Hagar put out his cigar. "Who do you reckon he is then?"

"He looks the same as a feller I knew in my days with the U.S. Marshals." Aaron rubbed his bearded chin and narrowed his eyes at Matt. "What's your name, son?"

"Matt," he replied slowly. "Matt Dawson."

"Dawson?" Aaron leaned back and smiled. "Matt Dawson from Colorado. Would that be Cripple Creek, Colorado?"

"That's where I'm from!" Matt sat upright.

"And do you know a Clem Dawson?" Aaron asked with narrowed eyes.

"He's my uncle," Matt replied cautiously. "My pa's younger brother."

"You're Garrett Dawson's son." Aaron's eyes widened.

"I am." Matt nodded.

CHAPTER 24

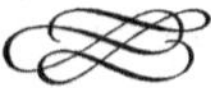

The last rays of the setting sun cast a blood red swath across the western sky. Matt stepped out of the sheriff's office with the gray-haired bounty hunter Aaron Steele right behind him.

The Texas Rangers had begun to head out of town, leading the long line of what remained of Big Billy Branson's Hell Riders behind them.

"What'll happen to them now?" Matt asked Steele.

"Most of them will be stretchin' hemp for murder," the older man replied. "The younger ones will get fifteen to twenty years of hard labor in a chain gang, workin' the railroad somewhere."

"And what'll happen to me?" Matt asked cautiously.

"You'd have shared their fate..." Steele told him. "If you hadn't been of such great help to the Rangers. And though I don't believe any of that hostage bull your purty young lady friend was spewin' back there, I reckon you joinin' up with murderous outlaws does call for some righteous retribution."

"Like what?" Matt eyed the older man warily.

"Here's the deal, son." The bounty hunter leaned closer to him. "And this too is 'cause you're the nephew of an old dear friend. I want you to ride with me for some time… I could use a man of your skills on a few jobs I need to undertake. And after that I'll get you a full pardon."

"What kind of jobs?"

"Bounty hunting," Steele replied. "Plenty of mangy coyotes out there with bounties on their heads waiting to be collected, and I could use an extra pair of hands and guns."

"Why in tarnation would I want to go bounty huntin'?" Matt took a step back.

"Cause it's better'n breakin' rocks on the railroad for a year, son," the older man growled. "And besides, you might learn somethin'. I heard you say you're lookin' for someone. Who is it and how long have you been lookin'?

"I'm lookin' for a man…"Matt said. "A man who… did me wrong?"

"What's his name, son?"

"You'd not heard of him." Matt shook his head.

"Spit it out, boy." Steele gritted his teeth.

"Shute. His name's Ned Shute."

"Never heard of 'im." Steele shook his head.

"Yep." Matt nodded with a whimsical smile.

"And how long you been lookin' for this varmint?" the older man asked.

"Since he…" Matt sighed deeply. "About four months."

"That long, 'ey?" Steele raised his brows. "I reckon it takes that long sometimes."

"How long does it take a bounty hunter to find someone?"

"Depends on how good the bounty hunter is, or how much the bounty is!"

"How long does it take you?" Matt furrowed his brow at the man.

"A week." Steele shrugged. "Ten days at most."

"Horse feathers!" Matt exclaimed. "You must be the best bounty hunter around."

"Folks know my name, here and there-abouts." The bounty hunter shrugged.

"Aaron Steele, the greatest bounty hunter of legend." Matt made a wide-eyed face.

"Yeah, somethin' like that."

'Somethin' like that." Matt nodded with a wide grin.

"So you aimin' to learn how it's done?" Steele narrowed his eyes at Matt.

"I ain't got no other choice, have I?" Matt said with a smirk.

"No,"

"Well, that's what I thought."

"Yep, and cause you're Clem's nephew." Aaron Steele peered over the horizon. "Clem was like a brother to me."

"Paw never did talk much about Uncle Clem," Matt said with a saddened expression.

"That's cause your pa didn't like his younger brother signing up to be a lawman."

"Pa wanted Uncle Clem to help around the ranch after Gramps died."

"I miss ol' Clem." Aaron Steele sighed. "You're almost a dead ringer for him, you know."

"How did he...?"

"We were ambushed, at the Tex-Mex border, taken plumb by surprise. We were betrayed that night by a darn coyote we trusted." The tall bounty hunter stared blankly ahead. "Been ten years now since..."

"I'm sorry I didn't know my uncle well...." Matt sighed. "He sounds like a real hero."

"That he was," Steele said with a smile. "And also, a darn idiot who didn't know how to keep his head low. But enough of that old sentimental jaw wobblin'. Now tell me, son... what did the coyote you're after do to you?"

"He... killed my brother, Tommy..." Matt replied, swallowing down the lump in his throat. "In cold blood."

"I'm sorry for your terrible loss, son." Steele placed his hand on Matt's shoulder. "And you've been after this Shute feller for months now?"

"He's always a few steps ahead of me." Matt nodded. "I find out where he is, and then when I get there, he's gone."

"Just a matter of luck," Steele said somberly. "But more'n that, trackin' a man down takes skill and temperament."

"I reckon I've been doin' pretty well on that account."

"You reckon?" The bounty hunter smiled. "In four months, a good bounty hunter'd track down a dozen varmints."

"What do you reckon I'm doin' wrong?" Matt sighed deeply.

"For starters, it's emotional..." Steele shook his head. "And I ain't faultin' you for that. But you've got to learn to control your feelings, keep 'em hogtied and out of the way of focusin' on the job."

"But it ain't a job..." Matt protested weakly. "It is personal."

"My point exactly, son." The older man nodded. "You can't make it personal. Personal don't let you think with a cool and level head."

"Well, now that I'm stuck with you for a while..."

"Dang right you are, boy..." Steele grinned slightly. "You might just learn somethin' while you're at it. Now com'n, I hear that cantina there serves some mighty fine beans in pork gravy, and I'm starvin'.

CHAPTER 25

$\mathcal{I}$t had been a whole two weeks that Matt rode with the bounty hunter of renown, Aaron Steele. They were yet to collect on any bounty. Fact was Matt didn't even know who Steele might be after.

They just rode for days on dusty trails, stopping at small towns and settlements along the way. If he knew his directions well, Matt deduced they were heading farther west and into Arizona, in the opposite direction of where Ned Shute was supposed to be.

If the Hoskins brothers of the Hell Riders were to be believed, Shute could be halfway across Louisiana by now.

The town they rode into next was small. It did have a livery and a saloon though. Steele urged his black stallion right on to the local sheriff's office. He gestured Matt to wait outside, dismounted, and walked right in.

He was out moments later, followed by a tall, slender man with a sheriff's gold star on his coat pocket. The man was smiling and shaking Steele's hand.

"Godspeed, Marshal Steele." Matt's sharp ears picked up the hushed tone of the sheriff. "May the Almighty watch over you."

"And you, Sheriff," Steele replied in equally soft tones. "This time, that varmint's well and truly in the bag."

Matt waited for Steele to mount up and then threw him a questioning glance.

"Let's get the horses rested and fed." Steele pointed at the livery. "And then grab us a drink and somethin' to eat at the saloon."

"Sounds good to me." Matt nodded. "And after that?"

"It's back on the trail…" Steele replied.

"Who are we after?" Matt asked.

"Didn't I tell you…?" the older man muttered, looking away.

"No." Matt shook his head.

"I reckon I did." Steele eased his big black toward the livery. "You probably weren't listenin'."

"Well, tell me again." Matt furrowed his brow and insisted.

"Names Elijah Hodge." Steele dismounted and handed the reins over to the stable master. "Wanted for multiple counts of robbery and a couple of murders."

"Sounds like he'd fit right in with the Hell Riders." Matt dismounted and walked after Steele.

"This hombre would mop the floor with all of them pansies," Steele growled as he tossed the stable master a few coins.

"That much mean, is he?" Matt nodded. "And you're going to collect on the bounty on his head?"

"I reckon I'm the only one who can." The older man nodded.

"Is he alone… this mean ol' outlaw?"

"He'll have a few runts doin' his biddin'," Steele replied and pushed open the swinging doors of the saloon. "I'll leave them to you."

"You want me to shoot 'em dead?"

"The bounty's the same either way."

"How much is it?" Matt peered at the bounty hunter.

"Decent enough," the older man replied.

"Decent enough for Aaron Steele, the best bounty hunter of 'em all."

"You sure got some sass, boy." Steele smiled tightly. "Just like Clem."

"Dang, I wish I knew my uncle as much as you."

"He was a fine man, a mighty fine man," Steele said with a rueful smile. "And you can aspire to be like him."

"Maybe I will," Matt said softly. "Say, what're we havin'? I am darn near starvin' here."

"Steaks. Rib eye." Steele had a wide grin on his weather-beaten face.

"Whoa! Can we... can you pay for them?"

"It's on the house."

"For real? Goldarn it!" Matt laughed out loud. "You must be a hero in this here town."

"Elijah Hodge's been terrorizin' the good folks here a while now."

"And you're goin' to save the town from this mangy coyote." Matt nodded appreciatively. "Dang, you are the hero of..."

"That's enough of that, son," Steele said as the waitress set the smoking slabs of meat on the table before them. "Now enjoy your dinner. We got a long and hard ride ahead of us."

CHAPTER 26

The noon sun was high in the cloudless sky, beating down its blazing heat on anyone foolish enough to be outdoors. The trail they were on looked like no one had ridden through there in years. Matt wondered if they were even on the right track.

He dismounted and walked up to where Aaron Steele was kneeling on the ground and sifting his hand through the dust. Not a horseshoe mark was in sight, nor any tracks of a wagon wheel on the hard and dry earth under them.

"A horse or two rode down this way," Steele said as he held up what looked like a piece of rock and took a whiff of it.

"I don't see no tracks… or hoof marks?" Matt peered hard at the ground before him.

"Ground's too hard to leave tracks on," Steele replied and took a bite at the little rock he was holding. "This here is a piece of dried horse dung. Two days old I reckon, from the smell and taste of it."

Matt jerked backward. "You just… took a bite of prairie coal?"

"It's sun dried." Steele shrugged. "Tastes like bad tobacco."

"And… and how do you know which way the horse was headed?"

"By lookin' at these shrubs growing along the trail," Steele replied. "Look, the leaves were nibbled by the horses, and the way the branches are broken tell us the direction the horse was going as it chewed on the leaves, draggin' on the branch until it broke."

"You can tell all of that by lookin' at some broken bushes?" Matt stared wide eyed at the older man.

"And so can you, son," Steele told him with a grin. "Keep your eyes and ears open, look for the signs, and you can read the trail like an open book."

"And you know for sure this is Hodge?"

"Only he and his three friends were the ones that rode away from town two days ago." The bounty hunter said as he scanned the horizon. "There'll be a small creek up ahead on the trail. The ground near the water's edge is softer, and I reckon we can find some tracks there, if'n they watered their horses."

"How far ahead is this creek?"

"The nearest bend is about a mile west." Steele leaped onto his saddle and kicked the big black into a gallop. "Come on."

They rode for fifteen minutes before the horses began to get excited by the smell of fresh water. Matt stared at the bounty hunter on his galloping horse ahead in admiration. He wished he'd have known Aaron Steele from before. They could have tracked down and gotten Ned Shute months ago.

"There's the creek," Steele called out and reined his horse into a canter. "And there, that's where their horses were watered."

Matt couldn't see any tracks on the banks of the creek, but he took the bounty hunter's word for it. Steele dismounted and led his great black stallion to the water and let the thirsting beast drink its fill. Matt followed the older man's example, patting his gray gelding's lathered back as it lustily drank.

"Hold the reins, son." Steele tossed his horse's reins at Matt and walked up the creek.

Matt watched the bounty hunter as he kneeled beside the stream and examined the muddy banks. He seemed to be nodding his head and talking to himself. Matt wondered if that was a bounty hunter thing or if Aaron Steele was communicating with the spirits of nature.

"Look here, boy." Steele gestured at what he was seeing. "Horseshoe tracks… and one hoof without a shoe."

"What does that mean?" Matt asked, peering hard at what the older man was pointing to.

"That's Hodge's ride. How would I know, I hear you thinkin'." Steele gave him a knowing smile and pulled out a horseshoe from his coat pocket. "One of the outlaws' horse's kicked a shoe back in town, and it was Hodge's."

"Do the marks match the shoe you're holdin'?"

"Like butter meltin' on fresh baked rye bread." Steele grinned and stood up. "And they're headed thataway. We're on the right trail."

"How far west are we goin'?" Matt inquired. "We could ride right into California at this rate."

"Nope." Steele shook his head. "We ain't that far west yet. And besides, the trail is veerin' off north now."

"So, we're headin' toward…"

"North of Arizona, probably up to the Utah border."

"You reckon this Hodge feller is aimin' to hide out in Utah territory?"

"Nope, I'm thinkin' he'd be holdin' out in some of them hills over yonder."

"How can you tell?" Matt peered at the faint line of hills in the distance.

"The trail leads there, with nothin' else to head for." Steele held his hand out in the direction. "And besides, see that thin wisp of smoke there, that's a cook fire."

"I can't see any wisp of smo—" Matt peered harder. "No, wait.

You're right. I reckon I do see smoke… but how do you know it's a cook fire?"

"Why else would anyone light a fire in the middle of the darn afternoon?"

"I reckon… I should be takin' all of this in account…"

"You're young yet, son." The bounty hunter smiled. "You have a lot to learn. So far, you're doin' mighty fine. And keep askin' all those questions. A mind fixin' to learn must ask a lot of questions."

"I hear you, pardner." Matt nodded. "Do you reckon those coyotes there can see us?"

"Nope." Steele shook his head. "I reckon they think no one can ever find them out here in this hell."

"Then we can get the jump on them right now."

"Nope, not right now. We can't ride up too close for them to see us in broad daylight," the older man replied. "We'll have to wait till dark and pray they're confident enough not to have a lookout."

CHAPTER 27

Steele moved in the cover of darkness like a cougar's shadow. Matt almost lost sight of the man a few times as he ran a few paces behind him along the rocky trail toward the hills.

Their horses were tethered about half a mile away, and they'd run the rest of the way on foot. The cook fire that had given off the smoke trail was cold and dead.

The bounty hunter gestured with his thumb at a little cave opening among the hills surrounding them.

"You reckon they're…" Matt whispered.

"In there." Steele nodded.

Silent as a mountain lion, Steele slid into the cave. A very low fire burned in the far corner, and the distinct shapes of three men lay asleep wrapped in blankets. Placing a finger on his lips, Steele drew his Colt Peacemaker and clubbed the first of the bundled men on the head. With a muffled groan, the outlaw twitched and then lay very still.

With a nod at Matt, the bounty hunter did the same to the next man, and Matt whipped out his gun and clubbed the one close to him. The fourth bedroll in the cave was empty. One of the outlaws was missing.

"Hodge ain't here," Steele whispered.

"Where is he?" Matt whispered back, glancing over his shoulder behind him.

"Probably out relievin' himself."

"You reckon he heard us comin' and bolted."

"It's possible." Steele prodded at the empty bedroll. "Looks like he slept nary at all."

"So, what now?" Matt stared at the bounty hunter.

"We gag and hogtie these three and load 'em onto their horses," Steele replied calm as a lake in winter. "Then look for signs to show us where Hodge is."

Matt nodded and grabbed at a length of rope from the cave floor. He tied all three men the way he'd been wrangling cattle back on the family ranch. He felt suddenly homesick but pushed that emotion away as soon as it hit him.

"Mighty fine work, cattleman." Steele laughed and hauled up two of the bound outlaws at once. "Now, let's get these varmints mounted up."

Matt lifted the third unconscious outlaw and followed the tall bounty hunter outside. A gunshot made him drop the outlaw and dive for cover. He crawled onto his hands and knees and peered outside.

"That's as far as you go, lawman." The gruff voice echoed outside the cave's entrance.

"I reckon I have miles more to go, Hodge." Aaron Steele's tone was as cold as his name.

"Yep, hell is miles down, all right." The outlaw laughed. "And I have your ticket to ride there right here."

"That's funny," Steele replied. "I have the same ticket for you here in my holster."

"Funny, is it?" Hodge cocked the hammer of his pistol. "Let's make it funnier with a hole in your head, Marshal."

"Killin' a US Marshal will make you the most wanted man in the country, Hodge."

"Pappy always wanted the whole darn country to know my name."

"You goin' to murder me in cold blood, Elijah?"

"You know darn well I am, Marshal Aaron Steele." Elijah Hodge hardened his tone. "And once you get there, you tell the devil to keep my seat warm in his saloon down in hades."

Matt had his hands on the hilts of this Colt Peacemakers, but he couldn't even see Hodge from where he was hiding. And he knew if he made a move, Hodge would fill the bounty hunter full of holes even before Matt could draw his guns.

He waited and watched. He could see Steele from his hiding place. The bounty hunter had his hands out wide, waiting for Hodge to make the shot.

"Give my regards to your pal Dawson," Hodge said before firing his gun.

Matt was taken aback by his name being mentioned. He watched, frozen into inaction, as Aaron Steele dropped down to his left knee, drawing his gun and firing in the same motion. Matt heard Hodge gasp and then the sound of a body falling. Steele was up on his feet, smoking gun still in hand.

"Is he…?" Matt took a step toward the bounty hunter.

"Dead." Steele nodded and holstered his gun. "Same bounty, alive or not. No loss here."

"What did he mean by 'your pal Dawson'?" Matt asked in astonishment. "How did he know about me…?"

"He was talkin' about your uncle."

"You mean Hodge killed Uncle Clem?"

"No, but he was with the gang that ambushed us that night."

"So, this was personal?" Matt eyed the fallen outlaw.

"In a way." Steele nodded. "But mostly professional?"

"How so?"

"I'm collectin' on the bounty," the older man growled. "Now come on. Enough with your jawin'. We have a long ride back to town with four horse loads of trash to cash in."

CHAPTER 28

The town was a small one, near the northern Texas border with Oklahoma. Matt stood outside the local sheriff's office, casually taking note of the three wanted posters on the wall. Ned Shute was not on any of them.

The three men on the posters were brothers. Buster, Larry, and Mordecai. The infamous Burton brothers. Each had a bounty of five hundred dollars on his head. And the bounty went up to an even two thousand for all three together. So far, not one had been collected.

The last three months were life changing for Matt. Riding with Aaron Steele was a learning experience he would never have gotten on his own, or with any other lawman, for that matter. He felt a kinship for the man, as if Aaron Steele was his own uncle.

Maybe Steele considered him as a nephew, or even as a son. Of the near seven months now since Matt was on the trail hunting down his brother's killer, these last three with the bounty hunter were by far the most rewarding.

"Come on, son." Aaron Steele's deep baritone cut into his thoughts. "We got ourselves a couple thousand dollars to collect."

"The Burton brothers?" Matt pointed at the wanted posters as Steele walked up to him.

"Yep." The bounty hunter grinned. "It's time for their robbin' and murderin' days to end."

"Where'd they be hidin'?" Matt asked as he handed the reins of the big black to the bounty hunter.

"They're holed up somewhere in the Indian Territory," Steele replied as he swung up into the saddle, "between Oklahoma and Arkansas."

"And we're just goin' to ride up and get them?" Matt leaped on the saddle of his tan gelding.

"Same as all the others," the older man said and nudged his horse toward the local saloon. "But first, we need to wet our whistles for a while."

"On the house again?" Matt grinned and licked his lips.

"It's good to be on the right side of the law, boy." Steele grinned back.

"That is until you get a blue whistler in the back," Matt said with a sigh.

"That's why it's so darn important to keep a calm head, and don't ever trust nobody."

"But… you trust me?"

"Don't bet on it, son." Steele bared his teeth. "And you better not trust me either."

"But I thought…" Matt was taken aback.

"Ain't you learned anythin' these few months with me, boy?" Aaron Steele narrowed his eyes into slits. "The world is a mean, unforgivin' place. You look out only for yourself, you hear… No one is goin' to have your back for you more'n maybe once or twice. You always be prepared for the worst. That way you ain't goin' to be taken by surprise."

"Well, I learned a lot from you, Aaron." Matt leaned back on his saddle. "And I'm much obliged for that."

"It's been my pleasure, son." Steele dismounted before the saloon porch and tethered his horse to the post.

"Another three months…" Matt slid off his saddle and followed the older man into the saloon, "and I'll be as good at hunting down outlaws as you."

"I reckon you would, son." Steele walked up to a table set up with a bottle of whiskey and two glasses. "It's good to have skills to take care of yourself in times of adversity. But I'd advise you to get on back home, find a nice gal, and settle down on the family ranch."

"I aim to do that." Matt sat himself down across the table. "Once I'm done with what I set out to do."

"This feller you're after, this Ned Shute…" Steele poured himself a glass of whiskey. "Ain't that good an outlaw to put a bounty on yet, I'd reckon. Nary seen his mug on any wanted poster anywhere."

"I had one on me," Matt said ruefully, "but I lost the darn poster before I joined up with the Hell Riders,"

"So, how're you fixin' to get him?"

"I was on his trail." Matt took a sip of whiskey. "Last I heard, Shute was headed for Louisiana. But then the Texas Rangers took out the Hell Riders, and here I am now with you for the last three months. I ain't got a cotton-pickin' clue where the darned coyote might be right now."

"He's a bad egg, son," Steele said, sipping his whiskey. "His sort more often than not always turn up somewhere or the other, when you're least expectin' it."

"I'll be needin' to keep my eye open for that." Matt nodded.

"Yep, keep both eyes open. It's important you're always prepared, son," the bounty hunter reiterated. "Keep a cool head at all times and be ready for anythin' anywhere."

"I reckon I am better at it than I was before," Matt replied. "And the more time I am with you, I can only keep gettin' better."

"That's darn good to hear." Steele nodded. "Now let's get some beans and rye into our starvin' bellies before headin' out north to bag us some outlaw brothers."

* * *

THE RIDE to the region where the Burton Brothers were last reported to have been seen took till sundown to reach. The border trading post with the Indian territories had a little cantina beside it, and the air around the place had a somber, foreboding feeling about it.

"I reckon our quarry is inside there," Aaron Steele said as he eased his horse forward. "Keep your eyes and ears peeled, son… These darn hombres are as mean as they come."

Matt nodded and dismounted after the bounty hunter. The older man calmly walked into the little cantina, and Matt stayed close on his heels. Inside, two men sat at one of the two small wooden tables, eating baked beans, and drinking tequila.

The third man stood by the counter, holding a knife up against the solitary lamp in the dingy room. The only woman there was standing over the cook fire, stirring a frying pan of beans.

It was too dark inside to see any of their faces clearly, but Matt could tell by the way they carried themselves that these three men, if not the Burton Brothers, were still wanted outlaws.

"Two bowls of beans and a bottle of tequila," Steele said to the woman who ran the cantina. "Make it quick, darlin', we're mighty hungry."

"Been long on the trail, pardner?" The man holding the knife asked without looking back.

"I reckon we have, friend," Steele replied as he sat down on the dusty bench.

"Where you headed?" the knife wielder asked and twirled the blade deftly in his scarred fingers.

129

"Any place where the coyotes we're hunting are," the bounty hunter told him.

"You're bounty hunters?" one of the two men seated across the room inquired.

"That would be right." Steele glanced in the man's direction.

"And who're you huntin'?" The knifeman turned around and leaned back with his elbows on the counter.

"Three darn outlaws," Steele said coldly. "Did they come this way?"

"What do you reckon they look like?"

"Mean and ugly sons of bitches, these ones are," Steele replied and rested his right hand on the handle of his Colt Peacemaker. "Wanted for robbery and murder, among other indecent deeds. They're goin' to hang these three once I turn 'em in."

"I reckon the bounty on their heads must be purty darn good to have the likes of you goin' for it, Steele?" The second man at the table stood up.

Matt jerked up. These three had to be the Burtons. Who else would know the bounty hunter by name? Steele threw him a glance, closing his eyes, indicating for Matt to keep calm.

"You got that right, pardner," Steele replied to the large outlaw and stood up. "Now we can do this your way, or we can do it my way."

"What is your way, lawman?" The knifeman growled and flipped the throwing blade in his hand, grabbing the pointed tip between thumb and forefinger.

"My way is to have you boys surrender yourselves and quietly come along with me." Steele nodded, his hand an inch above his gun.

"And what do you reckon is our way, lawman?" the one standing by the table asked.

"Your way is when I load your carcasses over your horses and ride back to town and collect on the bounty."

"We have a slight variation to that, Steele." The third one of the three outlaws, still seated at his table, laughed. "We load your corpse onto your horse and send it back to where you came from."

"You could try that. Mordecai." Steele narrowed his eyes. "If'n any of you three can outdraw my boy here."

Matt felt a jolt go through him as the three outlaws looked at him for the first time. His eyes had become accustomed to the dimness of the lamplight in the cantina, and Matt could recognize the men's faces from the wanted posters. They were the infamous Burton brothers.

"Say when?" the knife wielder yelled, and his knife hand moved back and shot forward in a blur.

Matt caught the glint of lamplight on the blade as it sped toward him. He drew both guns almost by reflex, firing from the hip. The blade shattered, and the knifeman went down with a hole between his eyes, his hand still reaching for the gun at his hip. Matt didn't wait to see the man fall. He was turning to his right by instinct, cocking and firing both his Peacemakers again.

The two Burtons at the table fell back onto the bench, their guns flying out of their twitching hands and their dark eyes widened with shock and terror. Matt holstered his gun even before the two outlaws hit the gravel floor, dead.

Heart pounding harder than he could remember, Matt quickly sat down before his knees could give. He glanced at Steele. The older man was calmly sipping his tequila. "A little warnin' would have helped," he said, his voice quivering a little.

"What for?" Steele drawled. "You did as I expected, even better."

"I could have been killed."

"Yep, one day you will."

"What?" Matt stared at the bounty hunter open mouthed. "No, I meant now…"

"Relax, son." Steele tipped his hat. "You did well… You remained calm, kept a level head, and were ready for it."

"I… I reckon I did…" Matt nodded and took a sip of his drink. "And now what?"

"Now we eat our beans, pay the nice lady for the food and damages, then ride on back with three corpses and collect the bounty."

"Two thousand dollars?"

"Yep." Steele nodded. "And you get half."

"You're givin' me a thousand dollars?" Matt raised his brows in surprise.

"Yep, son." The older man sighed. "I reckon you'll need it more than me."

"But we still have three months to…"

"No, we don't, Matt." Steele shook his head. "You're free to go. I ain't holdin' you to your sentence no more."

"But I…"

"You're goin' to do well, son. I darn right know you will." Aaron Steele stared at Matt with pride. "After we collect the bounty, you can ride with me to the Colorado border, and then we part ways."

"Well, I reckon I could go home." Matt nodded appreciatively. "I miss my pa, and the ranch. And Becky."

"Yep. You do that son," the bounty hunter said warmly. "Life is too short to waste away on vendettas."

"I reckon you're right." Matt stared into his bowl of beans. "But I promised Tommy, I'd avenge him…"

"And you will… if'n the Lord wills it." Steele stirred the beans in the bowl before him. "But no sense wastin' your life away, chasin' what might already be a ghost. Outlaws don't live to become old men too often."

"And neither do US Marshals." Matt looked up from his beans and narrowed his eyes at Steele. "Unless they pretend to be bounty hunters."

"You've a sharp mind, son."

"Why the ruse, Aaron?"

"Most folks, good or bad, shy away from badge-totin' lawmen." Steele shrugged. "But a bounty hunter can get to places, gather information, make deals… more'n any lawman ever can."

"That works on folks who you'd meet once in a while." Matt gave the older man a little smirk. "But bein' with you, I could figure out you're too darn good to be just a bounty hunter."

"How long have you known?"

"A while now." Matt sighed and pushed away his half-eaten meal. "I don't reckon a bounty hunter would go as far as you do. You have a passion to uphold the law. Bounty hunters do this for the money, but you… you do it from the goodness of your heart."

"I reckon I do." Steele grinned and stood up. "Now come on, son… let's get these coyotes back to town."

CHAPTER 29

A year to the day of Tommy's funeral, Matt stood with his father in front of his brother's tombstone as Becky laid a wreath of flowers. Three months had passed since Matt returned home, empty handed. Ned Shute still roamed the country and haunted his dreams every night since Matt's return home.

He put his arm around Becky as she came over to stand beside him. Their marriage date was set for three months from now. But Matt couldn't bring himself to look forward to it as much as he wanted.

Every day, he'd practice shooting his guns at targets. Every night, he'd dream of killing the man over and over with his bare hands. And though he fought the urge with every moral fiber of his being, it was not easy. It was never going to be easy.

The area around Cripple Creek had grown quite a bit since he'd been away. The population had swelled to almost twice of what it was. The gold rush brought in more and more people after the railroad was completed.

The town was growing quickly, and with it was the demand for food. The Dawson cattle ranch was geared up for a bountiful year, and possibly many more years of prosperity to come.

Matt rode back to town with Becky to get her safely home. She was a sight to behold when he had returned three months ago. He made a promise to himself then to never leave her again. She completed him, he felt, and more so now that he had learned so much about life and how he should treasure the rare, good moments it allows.

A ruckus over at the sheriff's office drew his attention as he rode away from Becky's place.

"You got to do somethin' Sheriff." A short fat man was yelling outside the sheriff's office. With him were several others who looked like prospectors and miners.

"I will," Sheriff Jeremiah P. Rawlins replied. "I will. I just don't have enough men now to go after those scallywags."

"What's goin' on?" Matt asked one of the miners as he eased his horse closer.

"We've been robbed," the man said bitterly. "A gang of mangy coyotes held us up and robbed us of our rightfully earned gold."

"Where?"

"Down by the mines, north of the creek."

"The sheriff doin' anythin' about it?" Matt eyed the old lawman.

"He says he ain't got enough men to go get them polecats," another of the miners told him.

"Yep, that's old leather-face Rawlins for you." Matt laughed.

"What about you, boy...?" The miner looked at Matt's holstered Colt Peacemakers. "You look like you could use them fancy guns in a firefight."

"I ain't no lawman." Matt shook his head.

"The sheriff could use a handy gunslinger like you, Dawson." Deputy Billy Grant walked up to him.

"And why should I help him...?" Matt stared hard at the young lawman. "He nary cared to help me when Tommy was killed."

"Oh, yes... your brother." The deputy took a deep breath. "I remember that day, still get the chills."

"Well, I'm headin' back home." Matt reined his horse to the right. "You boys best do your job now and serve justice to these poor gentlemen."

He didn't wait for the deputy's reply and nudged his horse into a gallop. He rode on for a while down the widening streets of the growing town before coming across another group of miners. These men were having a rather agitated conversation with one of the mayor's new assistants.

"The mayor better do somethin'," a red-faced man shouted. "It's the third time this month our gold's been robbed."

"And it's the same gang," another man added. "They're ridin' in and shootin' up the place, grabbin' our gold…"

"And I know them from the wanted posters the sheriff showed us!" a tall man in a black coat shouted from the back. "It's Marv Mason and Ned Shute."

Matt almost fell off his horse. Ned Shute. Ned Shute was here in Cripple Creek, with a gang of robbers, harassing the hardworking miners and prospectors. He reined the horse around and headed back to the sheriff's office. When he reached it, the sheriff and his deputies were organizing a posse.

"Got room for one more?" he asked, dismounting hard.

"You're one of the Dawson boys." The sheriff eyed him curiously. "I don't reckon we need a showboatin' loudmouth in our posse."

"But Sheriff…" Deputy Billy Grant spoke up. "Matt's the fastest gun in Cripple Creek, hell, maybe in all of Colorado…"

"All right." Sheriff Rawlins shook his head. "But if he messes up, it's all on you, Billy."

"Much obliged, Sheriff." Matt tipped his hat at the old lawman.

"What made you change your mind?" Billy Grant whispered, taking Matt aside.

"I felt sorry for the hard-workin' miners," Matt replied solemnly. "It'd be a shame to not do anythin' about it."

"All right, men," the sheriff yelled. "The twelve of us should do. Mount up and keep your guns cocked. Let's head on out."

Matt kept to the back of the twelve horses riding out of town, heading north for the hills. He didn't want to look too eager on this hunt and draw the sheriff's attention to himself. And he was not too certain about finding Ned Shute yet.

What if he misheard that miner in the dark coat? But if he did find the man who murdered his brother, he felt certain he wouldn't think twice before gunning the varmint down.

The hills and caverns were teeming with men and women intent on finding that magical piece of rock to change their dull, drab poverty-ridden lives. Matt felt sorry for them.

Not everyone was born to a rich family that owned hundreds of acres of fertile ranch land. His life on the trail for nine months opened his eyes to the bad side of the world, and to the good.

The sheriff had stopped ahead and was talking to the miners and other workers crowding around. Matt held back at a distance. He didn't need to hear any more of what the miners had to say. Old Rawlins would tell them all about it anyway.

"Well, we have a darn infernal job ahead of us, boys," the sheriff said as the posse formed a tight circle around him. "None of the folks here know where the darn coyotes come from and where they disappear back to after they rob the miners… and since we ain't got us no tracker, we'll have to be doin' some old-fashioned searchin' through these goldarn hills."

"I can try findin' their tracks, Sheriff," Matt offered from the back.

"You? Cattle wrangler?" Rawlins gave him a curious look. "What the sam hill do you know about trackin'?"

"I learned a thing or two on my travels around the country." Matt dismounted off his horse. "First sign I see here is a mess of horseshoe marks made by them coyotes to throw us off their trail."

"And how can you tell that?" Rawlins eyed him with suspicion.

"Lookit these marks, Sheriff." Matt pointed to the ground. "The same horses have been goin' round in circles, makin' these confusin' tracks to fool anyone tryin' to find them."

"Right." Rawlins nodded. "I reckon you're the only one ain't fooled. So then tell us, tracker boy, which way you reckon they went?"

"Let's ride around these hills and look for bushes and shrubs with broken branches and stems." Matt gestured at the looming hillocks around them.

"The boy's gone plumb loco," one of the riders said to the others.

"He reckons broken branches robbed the miners," another said, making the others laugh.

"Cut that out," Sheriff Rawlins barked at the men. "Anyone here got a better way of findin' them coyotes? No? Then keep your teeth clamped down and let the man do his work."

"Much obliged, Sheriff." Matt grinned and gestured to the west. "The robbers went thataway."

"The bushes and shrubs tell you that?" the sheriff asked him.

"Yep, they did." Matt nodded.

"I've known a few who did their trackin' this way." The sheriff nodded. "And since neither of us here have a better option, I reckon we'll take the way you show us, Dawson."

"Follow me," Matt said and mounted his horse, nudging it to a canter.

The twelve-man posse rode on for a few miles. The sun was almost three-quarters of its way down. The hills widened to reveal a valley ahead, and Matt raised his hand to signal everyone to slow down to a trot.

If he read the signs right, fifteen to twenty horses were ridden through that pass down to the valley, not more than a day ago.

He reined in his horse to stop and turned around to face the sheriff.

"Well?" The older man rode up to him.

"I reckon there are near two dozen of them."

"That'll make it two to one in their favor."

"Yep." Matt nodded. "But if we take out their leaders quick, the rest might just fold."

"Are you a lawman too, boy?" The sheriff almost smiled. "I reckon you're quick with them Colts o' yours to nail at least six of them in a gunfight. Billy and I can take out another four between us."

"That'll leave at least ten to twelve for the rest of the posse," Matt concluded. "Almost a one to one. Fair odds I reckon."

"But we got to find them first, son."

"They're down in that valley, by that cave." Matt pointed in the direction. "I can see faint wisps of smoke rising, from cook fires, I'd reckon."

"And you know those are the robbers we're lookin' for?" Rawlins peered at where Matt pointed.

"Yep," he replied.

"Right." The sheriff nodded. "You know the best way to ambush them?"

"Wait till it's real dark and most of them are asleep." Matt gave the older man a smile. "Then we leave the horses here and go on foot. It's best we try to club 'em while they're asleep then hogtie the lot of them."

"Better'n any plan I can come up with," Jeremiah Rawlins grudgingly agreed. "Let's do it. I'll tell the boys."

CHAPTER 30

Under the darkness of a moonless night, Matt led the eleven other men silently through the valley. The cave was large enough for more than two dozen men, and maybe a family of bears. Bears were not around these parts any longer.

Matt found no tracks made by bears near there, but plenty of boot marks and horseshoe prints. The outlaws did little to hide their tracks here in their hideout.

Matt signalled for a halt near the entrance of the cave and gestured at the men to surround the place. He stepped into the darkness at the mouth of the cave. A faint glow of dying embers far inside at the back was the only source of light.

He could discern near to fifteen shapes rolled in bedding, asleep. The sound of snoring affirmed that those were indeed men and not decoys. He knew a few of the men were not there and wondered if they were outside among the hills, keeping watch.

Silent as stalking cougars, the sheriff led his men into the cave and began clubbing the sleeping outlaws with their rifle butts and pistol barrels. A few woke up before contact but were easily knocked out with a thump on the head.

"We got the lot of 'em, Sheriff," Deputy Billy Grant whispered. "But I reckon two of 'em's missin' on account of those two empty bedrolls."

"You think they saw us comin' and high tailed it out?" the sheriff asked Matt. "And left their lackeys asleep to keep us busy."

"I reckon that might be so, Sheriff." He nodded.

"All right, let's have the boys spread out in these hills and hunt them down." Rawlins stood upright and raised his voice. "There's no need for sneakin' around anymore..."

"They ain't outside, Sheriff," Matt said, pointing at a narrow opening at the back of the cave. "They've gone in there."

"You reckon?" Rawlins asked him.

"There're signs..." Matt pointed at the mossy ground just under the narrow crack in the cave wall. "Like that dragged boot mark."

"That'd be Marv Mason," Billy Grant offered. "He's got one bad foot."

"And the second set of boots?" Rawlins peered hard at where Matt pointed.

"I'm bettin' it's Ned Shute," he told the older man.

"Never heard of him," The sheriff replied then scratched his head. "Or maybe I have... Was it sometime last year...?"

"We need to go after them, Sheriff," Matt urged. "There may be a way out on the other side, and they'll be gettin' away."

"Right." The sheriff nodded. "Billy, you take charge here. Have the boys clean out the place, tie up these varmints and load them onto their horses."

"Will the two of you be enough...?" The deputy eyed Matt.

"I reckon between the sheriff and me"—Matt smiled at the young lawman—"them two outlaws ain't got a dang prayer."

The crack in the cave was large enough for one man to go through. Matt led the way with the sheriff close at his heels. After a while, the narrow cleft began to widen into a cavern.

More boot marks were visible along the dusty floor of the

cavern, lit up by a strange slimy substance on the walls of the cavern that glowed green.

"This the way to hell?" Sheriff Jeremiah Rawlins muttered.

"One of the ways, I'd reckon…" Matt whispered back. "If the roof falls down on our heads."

"Goldarn it, son," Rawlins growled. "There'll be no hell you can hide in, if you get me killed down here."

"No worry on that happenin', Sheriff." Matt waved ahead. "Look yonder, the cave's opening out there."

Gingerly the two stepped outside into the open. It looked the same as the other side they had entered from, apart from the taller trees. The boot marks were clearer now, leading on toward the tree line.

One set was clear and deep, while the other had one boot embedded deep while another boot mark left a dragged trail.

"That's Mason's bum foot all right." The sheriff nodded. "And they ain't far."

"Yep," Matt replied, cautiously approaching the tree line. "There they are."

Up ahead, seated on the banks of a little stream, were two men sharing a bottle between them.

"That's Marv Mason," the sheriff whispered. "I'd know his ugly face and bad foot anywhere."

"And the other one is Ned Shute," Matt replied in hushed voice. "I remember his face from that wanted poster Billy showed me."

"Well, what're we waitin' for?" Rawlins stood up. "Let's give them coyotes the good news."

"After you." Matt nodded and kept his hands close to his Colts.

"Well, lookee here." The sheriff leaped out in front of the two startled outlaws, his guns drawn. "Christmas came early."

"Horse feathers!" Mason yelled. "They found us…"

"Get down," Matt yelled and pushed the sheriff.

The bullet tore into the older man's shoulder and ripped out from the back in a spray of blood. His hand went numb, and he dropped his gun.

He fell to the ground, cursing loudly. Matt was amazed at the quickness and aim of the man who murdered his brother. If he hadn't pushed the sheriff, that bullet from Shute's gun would have blown the old lawman's brains out.

"That's far enough, Shute," Matt yelled as he dragged the cursing sheriff behind the cover of the rocks. "One more step and I'll drop you."

"Who are you, kid?" Ned Shute yelled back. "And how do you know my name?"

"I know you, Ned Shute," Matt replied. "I've been huntin' you for a whole darn year!"

"Why?" the outlaw asked calmly.

"You killed my brother in cold blood, you bastard." Matt felt the hairs on the back of his neck rising in anger. "You killed Tommy."

"I killed many brothers of a whole lot of men, and I killed those men too." Ned Shute sounded as cool as the morning breeze. "I nary cared to know their names."

"Last year… in Cripple Creek." Matt took a deep breath and focused on calming himself. "You were bein' fresh with Bec… with a lady in the restaurant. And my brother defended her, fought you fair and square, and you killed him in cold blood, before he even had a chance to draw."

"Ain't my fault if'n a man's slow on the draw." There was a hint of amusement in Shute's tone.

"You cheated," Matt said, fighting his emotions. "You shot him low and dirty."

"That's what all them losers say," Shute replied coldly, "before they die."

"He was just a kid, only nineteen…" Matt struggled to keep calm.

"Old enough to kill, old enough to die." Shute let out a raspy, grating laugh.

"You'll be burnin' in hell for that." Rawlins wheezed from where he lay bleeding.

"I can't argue with that." Matt nodded at the sheriff.

"Are you fixin' to jaw me to death," Shute raised his voice, "or are you goin' to step out like a man and challenge me?"

"Don't…" The sheriff gasped. "He's really quick…"

"So am I," Matt replied and moved into the open. "Cover me from the other one."

"All right, big talker." Ned Shute laughed at him. "Lessee if you can walk the way you talk."

"I don't aim to kill you, Ned," Matt said. "I did intend to for so long, but not anymore…"

"Enough talk," Shute snarled. "Draw."

Shute's hand was a blur of movement, drawing and cocking the hammer in one smooth move. But his gun didn't fire. Instead, it flew out of his hand.

Shute went down on his knees, clutching at his numbed right hand with his left. His eyes were widened orbs of disbelief.

"Thunderation!" Marv Mason exclaimed. "I never reckoned I'd see anyone faster'n you, Ned. I didn't even see the kid draw and shoot."

"That's right. I am faster, bigger, and better than you, Ned Shute," Matt said as he holstered his gun. "And as I was sayin', I ain't got the need to kill you myself anymore. You'll stand trial for murder, Shute… and the judge will pass your just sentence."

"But if he killed your brother…" Mason looked at Matt. "You're in the right to kill him."

"I ain't no murderer, pardner." Matt shook his head. "I'll watch him be tried and hung for Tommy's murder…"

A split second was all it took for Matt to drop on one knee to dodge the bullet that missed his head by inches. In the same instant, he drew and fired, blowing a hole in Ned Shute's forehead.

The man had a stunned look on his narrow face, his left hand still clutching at his gun in its holster, the barrel smoking through the cutaway hole at the bottom of the leather.

He dropped backward slowly, dead before he hit the ground.

Standing as still as the rocks around him, Matt exhaled deeply. It was done. He had avenged Tommy at long last. He should be celebrating, drowning himself in whiskey and galloping his horse through Cripple Creek with wild abandon. And yet he felt a weight come down upon him like never before. His boots felt like lead shackles, his gun belt weighed down like a bullock's harness.

Emptiness filled his heart. Tommy was still dead. Killing Shute did nothing to ease the pain of Matt's deep loss.

"That was… self-defense, I reckon." Sheriff Jeremiah P. Rawlins crawled out from the cave; his shirt soaked in his own blood. "And you saw that too, Mason."

"If'n I testify to that," the weasel-faced outlaw ventured, "will the judge show me some leniency."

"I ain't the judge, boy…" Rawlins said gruffly as he tried to get to his feet. "But I can put in a good word for you."

"If you don't die of that wound first, old man." Mason grinned at the sheriff.

"This!" The sheriff laughed, touching his bleeding shoulder. "I've survived worse, boy. This ain't even going to slow me down."

Rawlins stood up straight, shook his head, and wheezed a little then sank down to his knees, fell face-first into the moss-covered ground, and passed out.

"The old fool's goin' to bleed to death." Mason had a smirk on his weasely face.

"Where are your horses?" Matt near demanded in a tone to chill the devil's blood.

"Behind that cave wall over yonder," the outlaw replied with a shudder.

"Get 'em saddled, Marv, and then help me with the sheriff," Matt told the man with the bad left foot. "We got a long ride back to Cripple Creek."

EPILOGUE

The moon was full that night, high up in the blue-black night sky, with the stars twinkling as they had since the beginning of time. Matt sat on the porch of his family home, sipping a cool glass of orange juice.

He leaned back on the broad bench and closed his eyes. The memory of that afternoon filled his mind once more, making him smile again.

Becky Johnson had looked like an angel floating down from heaven in her resplendent many-layered white wedding gown. She broke many a young man's heart that afternoon when she said those two special words to him that would unite their lives together—for better, for worse, for richer, for poorer, in sickness and in health, until death did them part.

He opened his eyes again to the stars above and took a deep breath, filling his senses with the sweet scent of home. Matt stood up at the sound of her soft footsteps approaching.

Turning slowly, he walked up to her, drinking in the beauty of her smile. Nothing else mattered to him at that moment in time.

"Mrs. Becky Dawson," he whispered as she slid her slender arms around his neck.

"Uh-huh, Mr. Matt Dawson." She looked deep into his eyes.

His lips brushed hers. She drew him into the kiss. Matt didn't care about anything else then. The world around them meant little for him as he drowned in the passion of their kiss. Then she pulled away, a slight frown on her lovely face. He raised a questioning eyebrow.

"Promise me you'll never go ridin' away ever again…" Becky whispered, "and leave me all alone and worryin' about you every night until you return."

"I promise, Becky." He stared into her eyes. "I promised you on the day I returned, and I promise you again now on this very special day in our lives. I'm never goin' to ever leave you alone… no matter what."

"I believe you, Matt." Her eyes misted and she grasped his arms tightly. "I can't live a day without you."

"I'm done chasin' around, Becky." He gazed deep into her eyes, reassuring her. "I got Tommy's killer, but as I told you then when I did it, and I say again now, it didn't feel anywhere as good as I reckoned it would. Nothin' changed by killin' Ned Shute, exceptin' for that coyote bein' dead. Tommy's gone. Gettin' his murderer didn't do anythin' to ease the loss."

"You did your best, Matt." Becky rested her head on his chest. "I reckon Tommy's mighty pleased with you… where he is."

"So, we'd all love to believe that, Becky." He kissed her forehead. "And that'll give us the will and the strength to move on and live our lives."

"We have a lot to live for." Becky said as they held hands and walked down the steps of the porch and onto the grass. "This ranch. The cattle business. Cripple Creek's growing every day… and the Dawson ranch will need lookin' after."

"Pa was sayin' the same thing to me the other day." Matt put his arm around her. "He wants me to take over runnin' the whole place soon."

"And you…?" Becky gave him a worried look.

"I'm done bein' a gunslinger, Becky." He gave her a warm smile. "You're the wife of a cattleman now. I'm puttin' away my guns for good. The life of a rancher is what I aim to be livin' till the end of my days."

"That makes me so glad." Becky snuggled up to him as they walked toward the back of the house.

"And soon my children will take over from me." He grinned at her.

"We'll have to get real busy then," she replied, blushing a little.

"What'll we be namin' our first born?" Matt smiled at his lovely bride.

"After your mother, if'n we have a girl." Becky gazed into his eyes.

"And if'n we have a boy?" he asked, holding her tight.

"Tommy," she said just as they walked up to his brother's tombstone.

Matt smiled and nodded, drawing her even closer to him and kissing her. He closed his eyes and offered a silent prayer, with the full moon shining down bright, casting a shimmering glow all around them.

The End

WOULD you consider leaving a review on Amazon? It would be appreciated.

More westerns are in the works...